THE TWELVE OF US

Tim Matthews is a practising lawyer working in London. He is married with two children and lives on the edge of the South Downs National Park, England.

THE TWELVE OF US

a novel by Tim Matthews

VANDINGS WAY HOUSE

THE TWELVE OF US

Tim Matthews

The moral right of Tim Matthews to be recognised as the author of this work has been asserted under the Copyright, Design and Patents Act 1998

Published by Vandings Way House

www.VandingsWayHouse.com

The poem *A Stranger's Smile* on page 31 is extracted from *Collected Poems* published by Vandings Way House © Tim Matthews

ISBN 978-0-9934437-0-1

A CIP catalogue record for this Book is available from the British Library

Typeset by Palimpsest Book Production Ltd, Falkirk, Stirlingshire
Printed by Bell & Bain Ltd, Glasgow

DEDICATIONS

I would like to thank Helen, Lydia and Will for all the advice and many suggestions which have helped me put this book together. Also thanks must go to Anna Bolter and Sarah Norris for helping me with the typing of the text. Many friends have given good advice and made suggestions on the story, Mike and Jane Whitton, Marcus and Karen Panchaud to mention just a few. Thank you to Mary Broughton for your critical eye which was very much needed and also to all the team at Palimpsest Book Production. Finally, thank you to my two English teachers at school many years ago, Mr Maybanks and Miss Secombe. I was taught the relevance to us all of the power of the novel.

CONTENTS

PROLOGUE

It was not unusual, over its long history, for members of the Secret Intelligence Service to die whilst on active service. It was rare for an officer in the field to be asked by his commander to fake his own death and disappear, but Stewart Kilbride knew that it was a first for an officer to attend his own funeral in such circumstances.

Strangely, the experience was not that peculiar to him. He could hide and disguise, it depended on a person's own perception. For in this church, this place of worship, nobody had paid attention to him, and why would they? He had made sure of this in the way he looked that day.

Stewart was sat at the back of the church, beside a beautifully glazed window. It had the representation of a harp in one of its panels. Gazing up, it reminded Stewart of a tale he had been told in basic training. Alfred, the King of all England, a warrior and great intellect, was courageous enough to go into his mortal enemy's camp. Without a crown of gold or fine clothes, but with a harp, passing himself off as a wandering musician. He had little disguise, he did not hide his face or hair or even his voice, yet who he really was remained hidden from the Danes.

Stewart was able to hide in this way as well, training had helped with that and his disguise that day was subtle but complete. Although he was hidden, Stewart was unprepared for the intensity of the grief that he now saw. The agony on Angie's face. The silent contemplation from Alan and his slow manner. Edmund was weeping as he walked down the aisle, many present from the team were the same. Some, including Daniel, didn't seem to be there.

Oh, what suffering! What he had done here could not be repaired. Nationhood had always come first, as his own father had said to him. Even before friends – who have been deceived. Stewart looked across at Angie again. She was looking intently down at the stone floor and hardly moving at all. Stewart recalled a mission to Morocco many years back and an informant who ran a local market stall selling cloth and scarves. She had lost her husband, who was an agent of the Service. When Stewart arrived to meet her, in her own grief, the lady silently stared at the ground so that her face and body seemed to have merged with her merchandise. A personality was gone, consumed before his very eyes.

Stewart could not bear it any longer. Hardly anyone noticed him leaving, closing the heavy wooden door of St Stephen's behind him.

PART I: THE CHAPTERS

I. ALAN

The greatest thing in this world is to love and be loved back. That was what Alan used to say if you caught him in one of his ethereal moments, which happened frequently. He was the only one in the team who would talk on such a level.

'That's garbage. What if you don't love anyone?' Leon would ask.

'Then you have not lived,' Alan would say pompously. For a moment the others seemed to contemplate their life or imagined life – if such a thing could exist.

Alan's own reality was governed by structure. By rules and regulations, statutes and cases. His thoughts turned in times of crisis to his career. Certainly he had no love for his life as a lawyer and he was equally certain that law didn't love him. At least that was what he thought. Thinking time for Alan usually happened when he drove to St Stephen's church in Graysmere. Sundays would start with the noise of next door's retriever, always at eight and always loud. Alan would start with his coffee. It was usually her making it before – but then so many things were. The car was where he would do his thinking, and this particular Sunday he thought about work.

As he walked into the parish church, Alan felt that something was wrong. Approaching the west door, he saw that the cleaner was there, which was strange.

'Hullo, June,' he said, 'Can't keep away then?'

The question was left unanswered and instead she replied, 'Got to be nice for him, you know, for them people that will come and say their piece.'

'What do you mean?'

The broom was put to one side. 'Haven't you heard about Stewart?'

It was then that Alan first heard that Stewart Kilbride had been found dead and the answer to why he had been absent. Stewart, the one who was always so very punctual and reliable. Contacting Stewart other than through his private email didn't ever happen – it was something to do with him being a spook.

Alan had been told that there was something more to Stewart, more than just a civil servant. Angie only ever managed to extract out of him 'Diplomatic Service', when she asked Stewart about his overseas trips. Alan had his spy suspicions confirmed at the away game at Pine Street Town. Stewart arrived unusually late and was dropped quietly at the end of the farm track that led to the ground. It was not the car, nor even the presence of the uniformed driver, which caught Alan's eye. It was the driver's rapid and subtle salute before he drove away. Military deference, not subservient cabbie. It all then fell into place and made sense. The secrecy, the foreign trips, computer expertise, fluency in

Cantonese and four other languages. So Stewart was dead and his secrets went with him. Alan could never ask him about his work, although he knew the answer would be crafted so it was ambiguous.

Alan walked to the vicarage. This was at the other end of the church, behind the cedar tree. Sunday Matins was an hour away, the morning sunny and quiet. Alan's duties as warden could wait for the moment.

'I got the call from the police yesterday evening,' said Father Nev. Neville, the vicar of St Stephen's, was known as Father Nev, the name given to him by the parish cleaner from Cork. It was a funny name for such an evangelical man, but it had stuck.

'Found with just the Order of Service for last week on him,' he continued. 'Apparently nothing else on him.'

Alan, clearly puzzled, asked, 'But where . . . how?', trying to come to terms with what he had been told.

'Big mystery. Gatwick apparently and the police are not giving too much information as the case is being reviewed carefully, by the Foreign Office or Diplomatic Protection, something like that.' Father Nev turned to gather his sermon papers. 'The Order of Service is why they called me, they often call me, of course, but this was particularly sad.'

A lot of people did come that Sunday. Alan was unsure how many more would be at the funeral. Stewart seemed to have little in the way of family. In fact, not anything outside the Club, which he clearly loved. That day the people of the town came to seek peace, since one of their own had gone. Stewart had no links to the church and Alan thought he was probably non-religious. The same could be said of many who would come to that Sunday service and then also to the funeral. It was at that first service that looking around the church he started to feel the doubt in him. Before him he could see a mixture of emotions – respects being paid, genuine sadness. People probably wanting answers. Then it struck him – what answers would they get? Stewart was never coming back. He concentrated his thoughts on his dead friend.

Alan had known Stewart before he had arrived at the town, but in fact Alan knew so little about him. A man with the most breathtaking intelligence, as though he was always watching the world, ready to comment or to opine on any given subject. Compassionate, yes, he was that. In some ways compassion was written into his face, making it look older. There was sometimes an air of world-weariness about Stewart. Alan thought back to the team reading the weekend papers and asking Stewart if he could answer the final crossword questions that they were unable to fathom. He never did word games himself but would happily supply the answers – he could concentrate on the match and answer at the same time.

Alan often asked 'How do you know these things?' and Stewart would smile a contented smile. Alan wanted to follow it with a reference to a possible place of work where he had learnt this. It was however an unwritten rule of the team never to discuss work at a game. He so nearly asked Stewart that question right then. For the team, what happened during Monday to Friday ceased to exist on this weekend day. It was the way to get away from the ordinary world. This did depend on which team was visiting for the match. He remembered that particular day of the crossword pronouncement. The opposition was Goring-port, a team whose visit would initiate the closing and then the secure locking of the bar. It would remain locked until well after play. Alan would have to keep the visiting team, family members and supporters, from parking a variety of vans, tractors and scooters on the main outfield. They were also hard work to deal with on the pitch. 'Boring-port' was the league nickname for them. Quite why they played the game nobody really knew. All the principles that Alan acknowledged as being part of what made the game would go out of the window upon their arrival at the ground.

There was one particular incident involving Goring-port that Alan remembered well. He often spoke with Stewart about it. It involved a ball striking the old oak tree within the ground. Seen in photographs taken before the First World War, the tree was a symbol of the town. It featured on the signs of various pubs in the area. Its huge branches were also rumoured to be the last gallows used in the area in Victorian times, so it had a reputation. The local rules for playing the game with this majestic tree within the ground involved the principle that it was part of the boundary. In particular, no player could be given caught out if the ball hit the tree first.

However, during the visit of Goring-port the routine explanation of the local rules with regard to the tree prior to the match seemed to have been forgotten immediately by the visitors. The match itself started peacefully; Alan opened the batting and was soon striking the ball well around the green. Deckchairs had appeared by the boundary rope. Young couples with bottles of chilled wine sat on the grass, deep in conversation. Graysmere looked the quintessential English country town. Older residents wandered across the boundary rope, completely unaware of the sporting event taking place.

As the match went on, Alan confidently hit one particular ball high and fast towards the oak tree. Meanwhile, an opposing player fielding out near the tree was busy running, his eyes on the ball and accelerating towards the tree. Young couples turned to watch and all the town would have heard the rat-a-tat as the ball hit the branches of the tree before falling into the fielder's hands.

'Yesssss, good one, Mate, you got him out!' a Goring-port player shouted.

Alan turned to the umpire and spoke with some urgency. 'Ump, the ball hit the tree first, so . . . it can't be out?'

The umpire turned to the fielder striding across towards the pitch, busily engaged in exaggerated high fives. 'Did you catch it clean?' asked Ump.

There was silence as the fielder stared at Ump. Before the answer came, Alan knew he was back to the pavilion: 'I caught it clean as a whistle, Ump, nowhere near the tree.'

Ump was hard of hearing, so appeals always had to be delivered at high volume. He had to ask the fielder to clarify the point because of the distance from the pitch. If a fielding side said it missed the tree, Ump would accept this. Honesty and fairness underpinned the game. That was the way Alan played the game and so he could hardly contest the fielder's version of events. He slowly walked back to the changing area, his bat for the day now over.

It was not normally in his nature to seek confrontation, but Alan recalled how after the match finished (a draw as was usual with this opposition) he strode up to the opposition captain and gave him the benefit of his views on fair play in sport and life. It was then that the trouble began. The opposing captain, known affectionately by his teammates as 'Snatch', gathered his troops together and informed them that everyone should leave that instant. Snatch proceeded to walk to his own vehicle in the car park. This conveyance was none other than a large tractor with full ploughing gear at the back, lifted up in safe highway travel mode. This he drove across the town green, ploughshare now down and engaged. There followed hoots of derision from his teammates, now reaching their assortment of vehicles. Alan, for his part, ran after the farm vehicle screaming obscenities. The Goring-port team joined in the mêlée, which soon involved no less than seventeen players and, bizarrely, also some spectators. Nothing could change the fact that there was now a deep furrow that reached from the car park to the main road across the beautifully kept grass that was the town grounds.

The county committee heard the case the following Thursday. A variety of sanctions could have been put in place, although no one on the committee could actually recall what they were. The visitors to the green that day were in danger of being banned from the league. They were saved, strangely enough, by one of the oldest members of the town, who reminded Alan that for some years the Club had wanted to lay new draining across the green but could not afford the required land works. These plans involved a large trench connecting the Clubhouse drainage with the main sewer in the road. So peace was secured by the committee and the opposition lived to play another day. The Mayor even wrote to the opposing town thanking them for their generous gesture of free drainage work.

Alan recalled his own intervention and wondered why he had failed to show similar fortitude in his own life. That very Saturday evening with Julie at the restaurant had been an attempt at restoring a withering relationship. The evening started badly with the front of house forgetting the reservation and hastily finding a less good alternative table. Conversation was forced and Julie seemed preoccupied. The noisy office party was not the trigger for Julie's outburst; it was on its way well before that.

'They make quite a noise, don't they?' Alan said looking for conversation.

'Well, go and do something about it then. That's the trouble with you . . . be a man and go over there!'

Alan found it difficult to remember what happened next, except that at closing time he was alone, even the office revellers had gone. A young waiter, sympathetic enough to avoid sweeping his feet, cleaned up, placing chairs on top of tables. Julie's outburst, with the dramatic exit, was witnessed by most of the regulars. It was four months later that Julie finally left to go to her mother, effectively ending six years of marriage.

Alan had never expected to be alone at this age. The perceived unfairness of it made him withdrawn. With no children from his years with Julie, his thought was, simply, of the waste of it. Stewart had been his rock then and since. How would he cope now? His friend had been there for him, the guide through his own fuddled mind, the support unconditional and complete. All was collapsing around him. He worked hard at his faith, gave time to the church, but with no reward. As he looked around the church, the question inside his head was: How can there be a God? Well, if there was, he had treated Alan badly. That was his instinctive feeling. It stayed with him that day and into next few days. 'Funeral only and then that is it, I am not returning,' Alan decided. He would put his religion to rest at that church service once and for all.

Alan remembered Stewart talking about his lack of religion, in contrast to his mother and her faith. On the subject of hope and illusion Stewart would say, 'My mother always lived in hope, right through to the end, but what she had wanted and prayed for never came. It was all an illusion.'

Intrigued by this statement Alan asked, 'Are you saying prayer is an illusion? After all, it can bring great relief if you believe in what you are doing.' At this Stewart contemplated and then he replied, 'It's not the act of praying itself – that is available to all. It is the believing that a result will occur, that's the illusion.'

'Some pray for others and not just for themselves. It's not necessarily a selfish act,' Alan said indignantly. Stewart looked concerned, as if he had offended him in some way. 'I am not judging, I am not saying it's selfish. What you say is true enough, but those who pray are willing something which is not there.'

Alan saw in Stewart self-assurance and self-will. He was widely known to people but not many could say they really knew him. Stewart clearly enjoyed the companionship of the team but somehow remained apart from it. He seemed not to share his life with anyone. The only family member he ever spoke about was his late mother. It was only with Alan that he would divulge this information. Consequently, Alan could always confide in Stewart, there was trust. In fact, there was no other person that Alan could speak with so freely. Stewart was normally neutral and non-judgemental, but these were firm views expressed to Alan on the subject of faith and prayer. It was unusual for Stewart to expressly state such an opinion. On the question of faith, he wondered whether Stewart had been correct all along. If this was the case, then Alan could not get out of his head the conclusion that his own life had been part illusion. Now with Stewart gone, he was truly alone. So his search for a new soulmate would have to begin now. He had a life ahead of him and he felt alone. He did have the team, Alan thought about how they must also feel. He would call Tomas but first he was going to see Julie.

Julie now lived about five miles away. Alan remembered that she had a new partner living with her but he was going to go and call in anyway. He took his car and drove through various country lanes until he reached an attractive collection of cottages. Too small to call a village, the cottages were originally homes for those who held smallholdings under the local estate. The main estate building, a grand place, was now a conference and business centre. He saw her house ahead and parked under a tree at the end of the road. Alan walked the last fifty metres or so, wanting to clear his head. Would she just say that he had only come to drop his emotional baggage on her? Perhaps the timing would be bad – they might be having a meal. The house was small and terraced. There was an olive tree in the front garden. This looked not out of place in its surroundings, but Alan had always thought it strange. He knocked the door.

Julie, after a brief pause, opened the door. 'Alan?'

'Julie, look, sorry. I hope I am not disturbing things but I had to see you.'

'No, not at all. Come in.'

Alan felt Julie looked tired, with large dark pools under her eyes. She had been crying.

There was an attempt at small talk. Thought he would pop around as he was passing by this way, he had lied.

'How is John?' he then asked. She looked directly back at him with a critical face.

'Gone, well . . . he has fucked off actually, for good this time.'

'Oh, I see.'

It was a bad time for him to have come. Alan was about to leave when she spoke again.

'So things not great really – how about you?'

Alan came straight out with it.

'Julie, Stewart's dead.'

'Dead? When, how?'

'Well that's just it, nobody is sure and the information from the Police is poor . . . about everything basically. But he is not here, and I need him Julie.'

Alan lost some control with the expression in his last few words. Julie quickly sensed it. All emotional barriers melted away.

'Oh, my love, come here.'

Julie put her arms around him. Tenderness that had not been shared between them for as long as Alan could remember.

'I just feel so alone right now.'

'I am here Alan, all those years of marriage do mean something. I shall get us a drink and you are to tell me the whole story, every piece mind and nothing left out!'

There was an old sofa in a bay window at the back of the house, with a cashmere throw lying across the top. It looked all of a sudden comforting.

2. TOMAS

The phone rang just as Tomas was getting out of bed. The girl, Elena – if that was her real name – slowly groped for the cigarettes, which were left by a small white bedside lamp.

After the call the phone slipped out of Tomas's hand and clattered on the bedroom floor.

'Are you OK?' Elena asked.

'No, I don't think I am.' Tomas paused. 'A friend of mine, well, he is dead.' There was a prolonged silence. Tomas did not want to say more to her on the matter, neither did she have anything to say. How could she, she had known him for less than ten hours. 'Look – I think . . .' He stopped.

'Yes, I must go.' She responded to his polite and unsaid request with a hurried collection of minimal clothing. Tomas heard the door thud closed in the hall below, then silence. Tomas cried, sobbing at first but then with big tears dropping down his face. This surprised him, as he never saw himself as an emotional person.

Tomas had been called by some people the stereotypical South African settler. Tall, with an athlete's build and handsome, thick blond hair, he cut a striking figure. Being hired for modelling sessions on Savile Row helped pay for his postgraduate studies and the agency that hired him was all female. Some assumed it was therefore all girls and partying for him. Then one would perhaps think that he lived a playboy lifestyle devoid of emotion, in some kind of bohemian whirl. The reality was not so. Tomas pulled what was left of his cigarette packet towards him and lit his first of the day. Click, click went the lighter. It was the sun coming through the window that he noticed first. It cast a warm yellow light on his hands. On this beautiful morning he had found out his friend was dead. He felt so empty at that moment. Maybe he could speak to Angie next, he said he would do so on the phone. But not until the tears had gone. These he couldn't stop, so he held his hand to his face and cried again.

The bond that Tomas had with Stewart began with rapid exchanges of conversation in Afrikaans. Two men who could converse without being understood by others. The mutual love of the language catapulting them into jokes and revelry, smiles and laughter. Members of the team would get teased horribly in Afrikaans without being aware of it. Howls of laughter would ensue from them like two naughty boys in an apple orchard which was ready to be picked of its fruit. Each Saturday proved to be harvest time for their pranks. For Stewart it was a love of the language and daring to be different. For Tomas it was nostalgic banter. Tomas asked Stewart where he had learnt Afrikaans.

It was as a diplomat in Cape Town and J'burg. Being attached to the embassy, Stewart had had a very comfortable life. His task in the African continent was to infiltrate ultra-right-wing extremist groups and root out any British nationals amongst them, or funding them. Britain would then report to the South African government on any findings. Stewart was not sure what the United Kingdom got back in return and it was not in his power to ask or find out. What he did do was to play the part of the colonial civil service gentleman well and to gain the confidence of such fascist groups. This secondment to the British embassy lasted many years. It came after the long Hong Kong posting, where he played the game at another colonial club, the Royal. Stewart could regale stories of African life and African places, and then just as easily switch to tales of Asian gambling houses and parties. He would also talk about girls from both continents. Tomas was taken in by all this.

Tomas himself had come to British society from the outside, having left Durban in the 1980s. He was an impoverished student wanting to get away at a difficult time for his country and to find some hope in humanity. Postgraduate studies were completed in England and a position at an English public school followed soon afterwards. Bright and charming, he soon became a deputy house master. His particular house (bizarrely called 'School' House) was soon amongst the first choices of the parents of prospective new pupils. Dinner parties in the county would include lively conversation about the school's advantages over other establishments. A further topic would be whether a son or daughter had secured a place in School House. Tomas was a potential house master.

Tomas taught languages and also took sport – fortunately only Wednesday matches in summer, plus training and coaching. This arrangement left him free for the Club, which was his real passion. That was where he had met Stewart. It may have been the charm he had as an individual – Stewart certainly had that about him – or it may have been that his own isolated self had recognised a soulmate.

He had not expected to be lonely working in a teaching post, nor for that matter to be lonely in England, the place he had learnt of at home as being rich and busy with great opportunities – but not if you are an outsider. His fellow teachers were tolerable enough. He learnt over time that there was a strict social order in the staff room. Friendships were limited to the lower orders, whilst some remained out of reach. As the years went by, he progressed up the ladder. A change in role and accompanying seniority led to new interest from staff who were at first distant, the move to deputy house master securing the biggest change. He recalled the time when the Headmaster had congratulated him on his promotion.

'Well done, old boy!' the Head boomed in the main corridor. 'Well deserved!' He then lowered his voice and looked across to one side, as if looking at the school trophy cabinet, before resuming eye contact with Tomas. 'Find yourself a wife and, in due course, the world is your oyster!' he said with a knowledgable wink, and with that he strode off down the corridor.

So that was really it? Tomas was a little taken aback. He concluded that in the natural order of things, as represented by an English public school, house masters are required to be married. It made perfect sense. First, you set yourself the task of finding satisfied and contented parents. Then they could identify with that perfect unit when handing over their child to the house master and his wife. It was deluded, of course, and would not stand the test of time. It was that day, together with the Headmaster's corridor comment, which seemed afterwards to have marked a turning point in his life as a teacher. He realised that the idea of marriage had no appeal to him for cementing his life within a school. As a concept it made no sense to Tomas, particularly after his first sexual conquest of a fellow teacher and then a parent in quick succession. Both events were equally exciting as well as exhausting, but did not last.

'The trouble with you Tomas,' said one girlfriend, 'is that you don't believe in commitment. I do all the giving, you do the taking.'

It was true. From them he took. The giving part was the education he gave to the young people in his care. The pupils, as the school preferred to call them. Tomas was committed to them, their humour, their innocence and their talent. For he sincerely wanted them to have what he had always lacked in his own life – a sense of stability. The ironic thing was that Tomas slowly became unstable himself. Stewart was one of the very few people that he would confide in. From Stewart he sought help with alcohol. The drinking started almost without him knowing. The move from social drinking to over-drinking was dramatically swift. True, it would numb any feelings of loneliness that he may have had. He knew that Stewart did not touch drink and he wished he had his fortitude, for with Tomas drink could lead to aggression and then violence. An argument with a regular at a local pub one Thursday evening turned into a fist fight and made copy in the local newspaper. There was a dramatic banner headline in the paper:

TEACHER IN LOVE TRIANGLE THROWS
RIVAL THROUGH PUB WINDOW

Then followed the report of that night's activities at the pub by a local reporter. The prose relied heavily on witness comments. The paper had an exclusive story. It did its best in the prose to cover all aspects of human emotion on show that night, particularly jealousy. But then the paper's tragic story rather abruptly ended with an over inflated estimate of the total cost of damage.

The Headmaster called Tomas to his office early during the following week. 'Frankly, this is all very embarrassing and irregular,' said the Headmaster. It was the first time that Tomas had visited the Head's own office. Other meetings had always been held in rooms off the main staff offices. Tomas was sat at one end of a large cabinet-style table, which smelt of polish. 'What on earth do you think parents will think of a member of staff throwing a punch, causing damage – criminal damage mind –

and police being called. All over an argument about a woman, by all accounts. A married woman. Are you out of your mind?'

That last comment was all Tomas could remember of what was said at the meeting. His own welfare did not feature in the conversation, other than that last throw-away question. Tomas could recall no concern about him being expressed otherwise. The Headmaster's scolding instead covered areas such as the reputation of School House (Why not the whole school? thought Tomas) and his own standing within it, being in a senior position. The last-chance saloon was mentioned, and other such metaphors. Tomas left the office with its smell of furniture polish as quietly as he could whilst pondering over his future, as had been suggested by the Head.

In the end criminal charges, thankfully, were not pursued. A donation was made to the pub landlord for costs not covered by insurance. This included damage to a framed original publicity poster of a 1960s movie. The artwork was monochrome, in the French style. The landlord was a collector.

Tomas continued teaching for a while at the school but struggled first with anxiety and then, over some months, with depression. He correctly concluded that promotion to house master would not happen on the current Head's watch. The girl in the pub with Tomas returned to her husband. It seemed that some hidden Neolithic instincts had been fuelled by being fought over by menfolk in this way. Her passion reunited with her husband's jealousy. Oh, what a heady mix indeed!

* * *

Tomas had delivered his resignation to the Head only three days before Stewart's death. It was accepted without fuss. He had not had his mental condition diagnosed at that point and was perhaps not able to properly make such a decision. The timing was awful, of course; he had to do it then to be out by Christmas, when he would fly home to his parents. With Stewart now dead, he felt even lonelier. Tomas felt that he had to make the call to Angie to tell her, if she didn't already know. That made him feel worse. He knew that Angie loved Stewart and that it was reciprocated. Stewart seemed not to have any family of his own but surely the police had informed her? Everything suddenly seemed very dark. He looked at the bottle of wine, then the cigarettes. What would Stewart want me to do?

Tomas remembered some years back Stewart talking to him about a civil riot and revolt in Hong Kong during the time of British rule, but before he was stationed there. This was a series of bloody incidents with riots being suppressed aggressively by the local police. Stewart had made a comment to Tomas one Saturday at a match:

Life has to go on and we have to carry life's bags with us.

The conversation then was about the death of a local Chinese man whom Stewart's father had known. Tomas used to speak of it with Stewart afterwards, and over time got out of him the history of the incident. When he had described this to Tomas, it was clear that Stewart was affected by it. It was the very first time he had mentioned his father to Tomas, or indeed anyone in the team. There were British ex-pats as well as local casualties. The riot was instigated by students protesting about British rule of the Colony. Many were injured and many died in the riots, and also in hospital afterwards from injuries sustained in the battles that took place in the streets. But it was the words that Tomas remembered.

He walked over to the telephone. 'Angie, it's me, Tomas . . . Yes, I am OK, but look, I need to come over. Can we talk?' With that call he had arranged to give her the news. This would be the hardest thing for him to endure. Did he have the strength?

3. ANGIE

On that Sunday morning Angie had returned early from her daily run. She lived in a smallish flat in a dull grey apartment block. She quite fancied a country cottage with roses that grew up to the windows. That would have to wait, at least whilst she was working for the Met, so her home for now was dense suburban London. The locality was considered good and was frequented by City commuters. In fact, the area had been described by previous generations as *Metroland*. This name amused her. Her beat would be relatively mundane here, the second officer good company rather than critical protection.

Her jog took her around familiar areas.She was a creature of habit as far as fitness was concerned. The final sprint was through an attractive enough park; the recent blossom had fallen on the grass like snow, some pink as well as white. Angie decided that she liked the pink best, whilst looking at it sideways with her head turned, stretching tired legs in the warm-down. She was thinking about him then.

Angie had first met Stewart at firearms training. The Metropolitan Police often trained together with the Security Service (commonly known as MI5), but to do so with the Secret Intelligent Service (commonly known as MI6) was unusual. Stewart was on secondment to MI5 and so formed part of their contingent for the introduction to the automatic pistol. The attraction to Stewart was instant. Whilst relationships were positively discouraged amongst fellow police, here was a pairing of a police officer and a man who didn't officially exist.

The timing was fortunate as Angie was coming out of a long and unfulfilling relationship to which Stewart was the release. Although she didn't realise it at the time, Stewart had given her a new start, the type you read about in magazines but cannot believe happens in real life.

It was the pink blossom that made her think of a wedding. Now, Angie, careful, that's all too much to take in! It was too soon, she thought to herself; anyway she would have to tell him about the baby first.

Her smile remained for the short walk home, but it lifted away when she heard the sound of her home phone. She heard it ring when she was on the apartment stairs; it rang a second time as she walked in. She remembered looking at his photograph. She had instinctively felt the call was about him. The phone's ring itself sounded menacing.

* * *

After the call from Tomas, Angie had left the house, with no idea where she was going. Walking, that was what she was doing, fast at first and now measured. She must have walked for hours. The street lamps had started to flicker into their warm early evening glow. On she went, passing shops and houses, and people walking home. They were all coming towards her. She felt that she wanted to hit them. She wanted to shout at them, 'Get out of my way!' But no sound came out.

She finally stopped in front of a café with a photocopied daily menu in the window. As she entered, a bell sounded. There was no one there. Angie drew a chair towards her and gazed at the plastic tabletop. It was the table furthest from the door. There was a tropical plant, very overgrown, hanging down from a shelf. It needed dusting.

'Are you all right, my love?' The voice came from the café owner.

There was no answer from Angie. The man looked at her carefully as she stared at the table.

'Well, you are . . .' He paused. 'You are welcome here. If you want anything let me know.'

'Thank . . . you,' said Angie.

He had a kind face. She wanted to just fold over and die. Could she ask for tea? she thought.

'Could I have a cup of tea, please? It's just, you see, I . . .' Nothing further would come out.

'Now don't worry, my dear. Tea it is. I shall get it for you and bring it over. Then you can have some peace with your tea.'

He started to get the cup and saucer, a click and clack was heard from the counter.

The large steel water urn made a whistling noise as it came to the boil. She noticed it was hot in the room. It was a small place – it was just her and the man with the kind face and nobody else. He brought the tea over, together with a plate of chocolate brownies. 'I haven't, I don't have . . . any money with me. My purse is . . .'

'I understand. I kinda guessed when you came in. Just let me 'ave it when you next call in.' She looked into the tea and held the sides of the cup with both hands. Her thoughts began to gather and she looked around. The walls were painted ochre. The door of the café had a red half curtain that didn't match the walls. That pain came again in her chest.

The café owner turned the radio on. A sports commentary of some sort. He glanced over in her direction from behind the glass counter as he emptied out that day's sandwiches. 'I can turn it off if you want?'

'No, please, it's fine . . . it's OK.' But nothing was fine, nothing at all. Still in her running kit, a long way from home. Trying to find an answer. 'Where am I exactly?' she asked.

The café owner picked up a damp blue cloth and slowly cleaned his hands. 'Look, love, we are here, here in Uxbridge. Do you want me to call anyone? You can use my phone if you like.' He started to look very concerned. Perhaps he felt he wouldn't get paid after all. 'My wife, she is here in the kitchen, she could help?'

'No, that's kind, no . . . the tea is what I need, for the moment at least. Thank you, though.' Angie moved a brownie around the plate but could not bring herself to take a bite. She would stay here because for whatever reason she felt safe. The bell rang; a regular came in and nodded back to the prompt of 'Usual?' from the owner. It was then she noticed the clock. It was a quarter past nine and it was dark outside.

She would call her mother, that is what she would do. 'Excuse me, but may I use your phone after all?' The phone was brought over and Angie called her mother.

'Mum, it's me, it's Angela. Yes I am, well, not really. Can you come and get me? Uxbridge, yes, that's right. I'm fine but I need to get home and see you.'

Angie did not know the location of the café so she asked the owner, who was doing his best to appear not to listen in but answered the question very quickly. 'High Street, my dear, next to the cinema.'

About an hour must have passed before her mother arrived. Traffic horrendous, it had started to rain. Angie's mother sat opposite her and they spoke together about the earlier call at Angie's flat.

'You must come home with me now, Angela.' At this Angie stood up and moved forward, crying, into her mother's arms. She had shed no tears since the phone call over four hours ago. The concern in her mother's face and her tender embrace ended Angie's own brave denial of the consequences of that day's news delivered by a simple telephone call from a friend. They thanked and paid the café owner and drove to Angie's childhood home in Richmond.

* * *

So Angie awoke the next morning in her familiar room. There was a set of dolls in national costume on a shelf. The window looked out on to the garden, the diesel noise of taxis' engines could be heard in the distance.

The door opened slowly. 'What can I get you, darling?' It was delivered in hushed childlike tones.

But Angie had her own question as she got out of bed. 'Why were they not able to contact any next of kin? There must have been someone, or some person who would be told.'

'Your father is making calls at work this morning. He knows someone in the Foreign Office, so he will try and get some information for you.'

Angie looked out at the brick wall she used to climb on as a child. Mrs Hughes next door had called her a real tomboy. She used to jump over to the other side, catching a branch from the old apple tree to break her fall.

'Mum, I'm pregnant.'

Her mother paused. The answer was a surprise, but also a relief. 'I know, Angela.'

'You know?'

'Yes I could tell, and that's why we both want you here with us until things calm down a little.'

This was how her mother had always been. Always the same, non-judgmental and no fuss. A 'let's sort the problem' approach to life and one that she had so much wanted to emulate.

'You should arrange to see your GP, and we need to take advice on how to deal with the situation. You have had a shock,

29

so it's important that you rest from work for the moment.' Her mother would try anything to prevent her patrolling London's streets. Angie noted the use of 'we' but it made sense, for now anyway, she thought.

'Work don't know . . . about the baby, that is.'

'OK, but when were you going to tell them? Anyway that's by the way as you have to tell them what the problem is.' Angie was angry now. Her father was not here – why couldn't Dad afford to stay away from the City office for just one whole morning?

'Daddy had work to do, important work.' Her mother regretted the last two words almost as soon as she said them. Angie fumed.

'The baby is not the problem, it's me cast away like this. No one contacts me, that's the problem. Not even my father can be bothered!'

'You must try not to blame anyone. Your work colleagues were not to know, if that's what you mean.'

'I am hardly in a position to blame someone, for God's sake, what will that do? It will never bring him back.'

'Look dear, calm yourself, it will upset the baby.'

There was silence. She was right, of course. Angie looked towards the wall and could see herself reflected back in an ornate mirror. She looked awful, her eyes red against her pale face, with dark rings below them. She sighed, 'Mum, I need to call the station again, keep them up to date. Then I shall head back to the flat. I shall get a few things and spend some time back here.'

Her mother was visibly relieved. ' Yes, that's fine, of course. Would you like me to drive you?'

'No, I will get on the District line and bring my car back here.'

The Tube pulled out of Richmond station with a jolt. As Angie's carriage crossed the Thames, she looked out and remembered how excited that view down the river used to make her feel. The places where adventures could start. Now it looked dull and grey and she could see ugly smear marks in the mud near the river banks. Her particular carriage was full. A mother and child opposite caught her eye. The little boy smiled at her, then grabbed his mother and put his head in her lap. He was playing with a little boat, just like those you see in bathtubs. The mother of the child also smiled at her and kissed his tiny head. And it was then she saw it above the carriage window. Dismissed as merely an advert first, it was actually a poem. Of all places a Tube train, Angie thought. She looked up to read what was printed there. It read:

A Stranger's Smile

Just when you think nothing is there
You will find strength and shed despair.

For that kind glance from someone's mind
Means that you are amongst humankind.

And if you think they do not care
Think on what they may have to bear.

So share that smile which is your gift
Stand tall, move up, as change is swift.

This poem had a particular effect at that very moment. Angie was to read it again just before she got out at Earls Court. It did seem to lift her momentarily and gave her a sense of hope that she might see Stewart again. Could the whole of the last 48 hours have been some huge mistake? Her mind was wandering, different thoughts kept coming into her head. Angie even thought that she had seen Stewart walking on the other side of the Underground platform. Whoever it was had been hooded by a large coat. Strange thing to wear in the summer. Was it a man or a woman? The figure now walked away but had been looking in her direction. She changed Tube lines and continued with her journey.

It was a short walk from her destination Tube station to the block where she lived. She checked behind but there was nobody following her.

Back at the flat she checked her messages, the memory was full. She wanted to press the All Delete function for the hell of it – she didn't want to speak to anyone. She remembered back to the Tube carriage and the child with the little boat. Life to go on, so she let out a gentle sigh and sat down to listen. The next message was from Leon.

* * *

When Leon came to see her later, they spoke together for many hours. Angie was able to unburden herself. She told Leon how much Stewart had meant to her. This conversation seemed to help her and the explanation of her own thoughts seemed to order her mind. Angie recalled, 'Most of all he was a person that was always there for you. Like a favourite godfather; there never seemed to be other family or close contacts other than us in the Team.'

It was hard to keep her tears from falling. Leon moved to hold her hand: 'Look, if there is anything that I can do or help with in any way.' He held his hand to her face, and moved a tear away.

Angie looked at him and whispered to him, 'It's just all such a mystery that he can be taken away from us like this. It's all so strange and so sudden. I even sense, quite strongly, that he is still actually with us all.'

'I think that often comes with bereavement.' Leon was not sure about his last statement but it seemed to help. He too was unable to unravel why nobody, not even the authorities, seemed to know what exactly had happened to Stewart Kilbride.

The mystery of Stewart's death started to become more complex for her when Angie was visited by British intelligence officers for the first time. About two weeks or so had passed, the funeral had been and gone. Angie was at her flat when there was a ring at the door. It was early on a Saturday morning. She looked at the video entry screen. The camera revealed the figure of a

Woman Police Constable and another person not in uniform. On opening the door, she realised that the WPC was familiar.

'WPC Angela Sterling?'

'Yes. This officer would like to ask some questions, please.' The last word was delivered politely but firmly and with authority.

Angie presumed it must be concerning Stewart's effects or other arrangements in some way. 'Yes come in please.' She led the way in. They walked into the kitchen and Angie turned off the eggs on the hob. 'Please have a seat.'

After they had sat down at her kitchen table, the WPC continued, 'This is Sarah Maddock.' The second person was wearing black jeans and a leather jacket, and without prompting produced a Security Service ID card.

'Is this about Stewart?' asked Angie.

'Stewart Kilbride, yes. Look, may we speak with you about Stewart?' The officer looked concerned.

It was good that Angie was seated. During the next hour she learnt many things. First, that Stewart had in fact disappeared without a trace after not reporting in for duty. They presumed she knew of his service record in intelligence. Angie learnt that it was known that she and Stewart were *associated*, at least, that was how it was described. Angie had been under surveillance, that was clear now.

Angie interrupted then and decided to get to the point. 'Look, as I am associated, as you put it, I can ask the question – he is dead but why has the body had not been found?' Angie was angry, her emotions being stirred up again.

'We . . . the Security Service is now sure that the body actually found is not that of Stewart Kilbride. In fact, we now know that his name was not in fact Kilbride but Lee. He was Stewart Lee. We have no idea of his current whereabouts. Has he been in touch with you at all?'

Angie thought the question delivered speedily at the end of the explanation was absurd. 'No, he is dead! I was told, we were all told, he was dead. We have had his funeral, for God's sake.' Angie held her head. It was disconcerting to have this information and she also felt frightened. She thought again of the hooded figure. Was that you, Stewart?

'Yes, we know, but we have to tell you there is a possibility that he may try to contact you.'

'What? Are you saying he is still alive?'

'We don't know for sure.'

Angie directed her anger at the visitors: 'But you lot at Five are supposed to know these things! What the hell is going on? He is one of you.'

'We realise this is a shock.'

'Damned right it is. First, I discover my Stewart is dead. I learn this from someone else he knew, as it turned out. Nobody contacts me from authority even though you bloody well know we are *associated*. Now you come here telling me that he may be alive.'

'He was working on a particular project . . .'

'What project?'

'We cannot reveal that.'

'Oh, fine, don't tell me then!'

'We do ask, please, that if any contact is made, any sign or unusual occurrence, then please call us.'

Angie felt that this whole situation was an unusual occurrence but she didn't want to tell them about the figure at Earls Court, not yet anyway. He must have been on the train that day. Stewart had been with her before at various times to see her parents for Sunday lunch at the house in Richmond. It must have been him. But why was he watching her? In his own time he would explain. She pondered over what she would say if she did ever see him again. Her thoughts were interrupted.

'Now, WPC Sterling, contact can be made with WPC Jones if anything should happen.' The MI5 officer then continued much more quietly, almost in a whisper, 'Can we help you in any way, Angie?'

Angie suddenly realised – my bloody flat is fucking wired up by these bastards. Was this person helping her or simply trying to scare her? 'No, no thanks. I think I have had enough to think about already.' She felt all of a sudden calm, totally calm.

'Well, yes. If he contacts you, if anything happens, any detail, let us know. Also you must not tell anyone about this visit or what we have divulged to you. Thank you for your co-operation.'

With that they left. Angie decided that the first person who would know about her possible sighting of Stewart would be Stewart himself, and not instruments of the British State.

Why would he want this? Angie tried to think of things he had said or may have implied over the past weeks. There was nothing that she could recall. He was his usual self, calm and contemplative. There was nothing in his face that gave away any indication of or any objective to disappear. Angie then thought of her pregnancy – was there any way he would have known? Something left in her flat that might give it away – he had his own key after all. The testing kit in the bathroom, she suddenly remembered. Although she had partly hidden the box, nothing could be easier for him if he was looking for it. So for Angie the answer lay in whether or not he had been to the flat whilst she was away. If so, what was his own secret and had he found what he was searching for?

He had only been able to leave a message on the phone: 'Angie, it's me, Leon. Look, I've just heard the news. It's awful and I wanted to say how very sorry I am. If you need anything let me know.'

Leon was more than sorry, he was furious. Stewart had borrowed several thousand pounds from him and it was unsecured. There was no next of kin that anyone was aware of. This was damned inconvenient and he was going to be well stuck now. What started as an off-the-cuff remark at a match had led to a considerable loan in less than three months.

'I need a little something to get me over the line,' Stewart had said. 'I can't go to the bank, as I'm not a home owner . . . it's just for a short time until the end of the season, you understand.'

Not only was Stewart not a home owner, he didn't seem to have any home at all, not even a rental. Leon had tried all day to find out but Stewart was as good as unknown. He had traced a possible tenancy at Downs Road by making enquiries at a letting agency, and he would take a look there the next day. So

Downs Road Estate was his lead and someone had suggested number Eight in the main route to the estate.

Leon set off the next day to find the place. The wind caught his hair as he stepped out of his parked car. He was smaller than average in height and his hair was carefully combed in one direction. As he walked, the wind blew it out of shape. He gathered his hair with his hand and contemplated the scene.

The housing estate was set in a strange part of the town, separated by a junior school and its grounds from the main collection of town houses. Downs Road probably once was a lonely farm road but now was made up of Fifties-era houses on both sides. They looked tatty in contrast to the older homes in the town centre. Lawns here were unkept. Cars seemed to be either dented or on bricks in driveways.

Leon must have looked suspicious as he gazed up and down the road studying houses. An older lady pulling along her shopping in a wheeled bag stopped and eyed him closely. He was now directly outside a property with a small sign with the word eight written on it.

'You after more stuff?' the lady asked. It seemed a strange question for her to ask.

'I wanted to see where Stewart Kilbride lives, or lived rather. Did you know him?' Leon asked. The question was left open.

The lady continued, 'You better take all you want this time, don't keeping coming back for more.'

'What? So who has been here?' he asked.

'Those gentlemen in the van, I thought they had come for

the telephone fault, you know the BT.' She frowned, as if she was describing some hideous monster.

'So people have been here to take things away?'

'Yes, and took a load of stuff. I told them they should do it proper, with removal people, not in the middle of the night like that with a little van.'

'Is there anything left inside?' he asked, whilst peering in through a nearby window.

'Mostly all gone. They had to come again, mind. Something about a new basement.'

Leon felt he was on to something here. 'Look, I am a friend of Stewart and I need to have a look inside. Do you know who has the key?'

'They took the keys. I had a spare pair – just for cleaning, of course. I am from here, my garden backs on to his. Yes, they took the keys.' She looked at him for a moment.

Leon said his thanks and with a curt goodbye he gave her a card with his mobile number written on it. It was probably useless to do so, he thought. Stewart had clearly left nothing, nothing of value to him anyway. Anyway people had been there first. Perhaps he was some kind of spy after all, there were rumours about it.

'Look, if anything happens, if you find anything, let me know.'

She nodded.

'Mrs?' he asked.

'Miss Pennington,' she replied.

He travelled back and, feeling like an early drink, he stopped in at the White Horse pub.

'My God, you look pissed off!' the landlord remarked as he walked in.

'Yes well, you would be. That guy Stewart Kilbride has left this world with no money and he owes me a lot.'

'You mean Stewart Kilbride from the Club. Gosh, awful business that.'

'Well, you would think that he would have left something, I didn't have to lend him, you know – he was a friend. That was why I did it.' There was no reaction.

'The guys in here from the Club were well shocked when they found out,' he said, pouring a pint.

'Shocked? I bet they were. Not as shocked as me.' Leon had asked for the guest ale. He drank it quickly, but didn't feel any better.

The landlord continued, 'They are saying it was all very strange, you know the death and that, being investigated. Trouble is, I don't think he had family at all.'

'No,' said Leon. 'That he certainly did not have.'

There were cheers from a group at one end of the pub; it was an office night out. Leon looked up at the clock. 'Get me another drink, Ken.'

Oscar walked over to him. He was part of the party that night; it was time for more drinks. 'My word, you look well happy, Leon!'

'Don't you start!' He shook his friend's hand.

Oscar was surprised when Leon explained his loan arrangement and the attempt to find any trace of contacts or family. He was less surprised about the result of the visit to Stewart's house. Oscar explained that he thought the police were investigating his death and as part of that were taking his belongings.

'So you knew where he lived?' Leon was intrigued by this. 'You are about the only person who did!'

'I did go there once to help with some outside building work.'

Leon left later that evening and received a call as he walked into his house. He didn't recognise the number on his phone.

'It's me, about that there house you were looking at.'

'What – sorry?'

'You know you were looking there today . . . for Mr Kilbride?'

'Yes, oh yes.'

She continued, 'Well, it might not be much but I did find something when I was cleaning up there.'

'OK?'

'There was this tin of tea, jasmine tea. I saw no point leaving it, him being dead and all. Seemed a waste.'

Leon was on the point of confirming that it was nothing when she continued, 'There was this little thing in the tin, it fell out when I was using the tea. Well, I didn't know what it was but my son David says it's a computer stick. Weird one, but a computer stick for sure.'

Leon sensed this might be his only lead so it could be worth following. 'Can I come and see it? Yes, now.'

* * *

The tin was small and painted red, with birds of prey on it. Clearly an object that had been crafted, not just produced en masse. Leon collected the USB stick together with the tin from the lady's cottage. She seemed glad to be rid of it: 'Them birds on it give me the creeps,' she said when he left.

The type of bird was difficult to identify. Each had evil-looking claws which were well out of proportion to the body, but he thought nothing further of it. He took the USB stick and plugged it into his PC. A whole series of Chinese lettering opened up in front of him on the screen, obviously asking for a password. After a few minutes the screen went blank. He was locked out of whatever it was.

This made no sense at all. He tried again, but this time a series of audible signals were coming from his PC as if transmitting – he couldn't seem to stop it. As he looked at his PC, websites seemed to be opening on screen, one after another, like some weird video game. He was unable to exit any site that opened, and so after about twenty minutes Leon unplugged the power source and the PC ground to a halt. Silence at last. Leon removed the USB stick and let out a slow whistle. 'My goodness, Stewart Kilbride, what have you been up to?' He contemplated what he had found. It seemed innocent enough but he sensed danger. There could be some money in whatever was in that stick. Quite why he decided to hide it that evening was a mystery to him at the time, but it felt the right thing to do. Nobody would find it now.

Leon pulled a can of supermarket-branded lager from the fridge in his kitchen. He took it upstairs to the bedroom with him. Television on, he would contemplate world news for a while.

It was about 3am, well after he had gone to sleep, when his back door was silently accessed. An instant later he was rudely awoken, lying on his bedroom floor with a hand holding his head down on to the carpet.

'Your computer now, and fast. Show me where.'

'What the hell is this about?' shouted Leon.

'Shut up and show me your computer.' At least two others ran into the house, Leon could make them out with a sideways vision available to him.

'Well, put your gun down and I shall show you.' Leon surprised himself when the words were expressed calmly and slowly. He looked up and made eye contact with the intruder, who was dressed in black, with his legs and chest clad in some kind of modern military armour. Goodness only knows what he was expecting to meet here. He looked sinister, but there was some surprise in his expression.

The pistol he held was slowly placed in an oversized holster slung around his chest.

'After you,' said the soldier to Leon. Calm and authoritative. Shouting was over for now at least.

Leon knew the content of the USB stick was dangerous but this was pushing it to the limits. They wouldn't find it and so he was going to have to bluff it. He walked downstairs and opened the door to his basement study. He flicked a light switch and a fluorescent tube buzzed into life.

'Here is my PC. What the hell do you want it for?'

For a moment Leon thought some IT geek would appear out of nowhere and access all his files, instantly recalling his passwords and clearing his memory banks. In truth it was more direct than that. A metal mallet went through the PC screen, the back panels were broken open with a crowbar and the hard drive pulled out. The soldier who clearly was team leader said, 'That's it' or a similar phrase, and with that they left with the hardware.

'Stay for coffee if you like,' Leon shouted after them.

Leon took stock of the situation. Stewart Kilbride was clearly involved in something serious. He had borrowed a lot of money, which Leon needed back. He was going to find out, what and why exactly. These guys were armed ready for a minor battle, so the information was dangerous, very dangerous. He would go back to Stewart's house.

Leon waited a few days before venturing back to Stewart's house at 8 Downs Road. He stood outside there for some time until dusk had settled. There was nobody about, not even the old lady with her shopping this time. He opened the gate and went around the back of the house. Leon spotted the kitchen window, which was easy to force and within one minute he was in the house.

He walked around inside, allowing his eyes to adjust to the half-light. The place had been totally cleared, there was little left in the house that could help. Leon searched for papers, letters or other documents in fact anything that could be some kind of lead for him. But everything had gone, in fact Stewart's home had clearly been 'cleansed'. There were a few books, mostly paperback novels and some thick set language text books, plus an equally large history of the Second World War. Why Leon switched on his mini-flashlight at that point and stared at that particular book he wasn't sure. Then in his mind was a conversation Stewart had had with Alan at a game which Leon had overheard. It was about something trivial, like the answer to a puzzle or quiz question, perhaps a crossword clue. But Leon remembered the answer – *Anderson Shelter*. Stewart had made a remark then about how people have found them in gardens, even now, years after the war.

Leon took down volume one and went to the index. Chapter 2: 'The Home Front', page 56 was where he found the description with a small diagram of an Anderson shelter. Then came a sudden realisation. Stewart had said even in a quiet Home Counties commuter town such shelters and their rusty remains can be found. It was too dark now to look, he would wait for the weekend. Leon would come again and look in the garden. He tucked the book under his arm and left the way he had come.

When Leon returned to search the garden in daylight, he was initially disappointed. The plot was small and not well kept, with garden fences on each side and a wall at the back. At the wall end were the remnants of what looked like an old apple orchard covered with thick brambles. There was no shelter or other building visible. Where would an Anderson shelter be placed? He decided to look it up in the book he had brought it with him, to place back where it belonged. It gave him the answer. They would often be shared by neighbours; the Government encouraged this for cost-saving reasons. So it was likely to be at the end of the garden within the brambles, accessible by the then neighbours. Then Leon realised that the brick wall he could see at the end of the garden was the boundary with Miss Pennington. He would pay her another visit.

'A way through the wall? Well, yes, dear, it's like an old sort of hatch door. Mr Kilbride repaired it for me.'

'Can you show me? Hang on, first of all, did you tell the people who came to Stewart's house?'

'Tell them? They didn't ask me! The hatch thing is a good way for my cat to get in. She is always roaming around that old orchard. It was very sweet of Mr Kilbride! She can't jump up to the wall no more, you know.'

'Can I take a look?' Leon asked.

The old dear led him carefully outside. She noticed him looking at her immaculate garden. 'I have a young man who comes and helps, lovely boy he is too.'

She pointed to the wall. There slightly hidden at first view was the shape of a door. It looked like a priest door he had once seen in a stately home. The paint was peeling and had acquired the same colours as the wall through the vegetation attached to it. There at the bottom was a small cat flap. There seemed to be no latch or other way to open the door itself.

'I might have a look inside!' Leon said to Miss Pennington, who looked at him politely but quizzically.

'You put your hand through the flap, and you will feel a cord. Just pull it, dear.' With that she turned on her heels and slowly moved away. 'I shall be inside.' She went through the back door.

Leon put his hand through and felt for the cord. It was there but so was something else solid at the end of it. He turned back to the house. No sign of her. He took out the flashlight and shone the light on a toy mouse attached at the end of the cord. Of course! Leon smiled. With one sharp tug, a latch on the other side of the door was released and with it the door. Leon had to crawl through the opening.

It was dark, and he shone his light forward. There was an outline of what he was looking for – a shelter in the shape of a cylinder and one which had clearly been refurbished with new aluminium sheeting. He found an opening; strangely, there was no lock. Well, Leon thought, this is finally it. What have you got for me, Stewart? He shone the light inside. Computer equipment, hard drives and memory sticks. This time he could identify the sticks as very high-memory capacity units. Leon had struck gold at last. The first USB stick that Leon had found was clearly some kind of diversion. A teapot of all places! They must have found it on the first sweep and were waiting to summon Britain's military for the first poor sod who placed it in his PC. This here must be what they were trying to find. Leon thought quickly. He had the benefit of time, as no one knew he had this treasure trove. The Government would pay for this information but he had to plan it carefully.

Then he heard the noise of a gentle clatter on the roof of the shelter. He turned the light off. He was done for now, there was no explaining this collection he had uncovered. He then heard purring. It was Miss Pennington's cat. Leon sighed a long sigh of relief and returned to the old dear in the kitchen holding her companion.

'I went in to try and find your cat for you, and here she is.'

'Oh, you are such a dear. You know, I wondered why you went in there, all dark and that – I thought you had gone a bit mad, you know – but I have made the tea! You must come again, it is nice to have a man about the place every now and then. Please do come any time you want, you know.'

There was a glint in her eye, her face was old but the eyes seemed young still and were as bright as crystal. She would tell him in her own time, he presumed. For the moment he had what he wanted.

5. EDMUND

Edmund was the senior partner of the local GP practice. It covered what was essentially three towns and a quarter of one town. On a Saturday practically half of his own team was a patient. In some matches members of the opposition would be patients. Once during a match a bowler, who dramatically pulled up from his run-up took off his sock and asked what to do about the very heavy blistering on his foot. It looked quite grotesque out on the pitch, and strangely alien.

'We may need to take the foot off at the ankle.'

Well, why not? What the hell was he asking this for anyway? This was leisure time, for goodness' sake.

'You . . . you're not serious, are you?'

Ump intervened and asked the bowler to either retire or get on with it. The man replaced his sock and walked off.

Edmund was going to cheer him up in the bar later, but the poor fellow had left the ground early.

The game was for him relaxation and also release. The green itself was exceptionally beautiful, typically English, with each feature that conjured up the picture-postcard idyllic situation.

Church by the side, oak tree within the ground itself. A white-boarded pavilion with balcony and deckchairs. Duck pond. Beyond the pond was a large stone and flint-faced cottage. Ducks and even geese wandered aimlessly in its garden. This was Edmund's home.

Stewart was a patient. The first ever consultation he remembered involved advice on the safe removal of a tattoo. A strange set of symbols, which Stewart was keen to obliterate. It was Edmund who told him the Club were always looking for players. Edmund took Stewart to the first pre-season training and that was how it had started.

Edmund would say something on his behalf at the funeral, but not the truth. He was convinced that Stewart had faked his death. Stewart was not himself when they last met in that bar in Soho. Edmund remembered walking down Wardour Street with Stewart afterwards. Stewart suddenly stopped at the street's sign at the point where it met Leicester Square. He stared at the sign and became agitated.

'Edmund, look, I am going to have to leave. For a long time. Please don't ask why. It's not about you.'

'What? Well, how long this time?' Edmund asked.

'I don't know yet but you must never tell anyone. I shall let you know.'

'I guess it's your employer then. Official business? I don't know why you put up with it.'

The last words were left unanswered. Stewart looked again at the sign.

'Promise me, Ed. You cannot tell a soul.'

'In my capacity as your doctor or your lover? I am not, either ethically nor legally, able to be both!'

'This is serious, Ed.'

'So am I! On both counts. Why do you need to ask? Unless you have committed a crime?'

'No, well, not that kind of crime.'

'Then I shall tell nobody.'

Then he was supposedly found dead, although there was doubt about the body. But what did it all mean and where was he? That, he was determined to find out. It would need to be after the funeral. The funeral was difficult because that was when the pain had hit. Why has he, Edmund, been dispensed with in this way? The man he loved leaving him like this.

He would have to return his thoughts to that last evening back in London, it was the only way to make sense of it. He would go back to Wardour Street. It was late when Edmund caught the train up to Waterloo. He walked to Soho across the pedestrian bridge, the evening sun was poking through some dark clouds. The same mix of customers was at the bar. The bar manager was asked whether he had seen a man of Stewart's description recently. No was the answer. He even thought about asking the regulars but that would be too obvious. He left the bar as it started to rain. It was warm misty rain, merging into the light from the street lamps.

Edmund stood at the street sign, and thought again about what Stewart had said that night. Then he noticed the sign. Edmund couldn't be totally certain but there was something different about the Wardour Street sign. It was the translation alongside the designation *City of Westminster* – a visible strip had been placed across where the original Chinese characters had been. Now there were new characters, a stronger bolder black.

In the next few days calls were made to Westminster City Council and various answering machines listened to, until Edmund spoke to someone who seemed to know about the signs in that area. He said, 'Repairs were made to the Wardour Street south sign, or Eight Zero-Twelve as it is known, not that long ago. I remember it. Some joker had changed the final set of Chinese characters. Nobody reported it for some time. We then had a complaint from a local restaurant owner who knew the language and we discovered that it didn't mean City of Westminster at all, not one bit!'

'What did it say?'

'Look, why do you need know this? The change has been made, it was vandalism. Smart paintwork, mind, and he or she must have had access to the window nearby. There was nothing picked up by the CCTV, no ladders in Soho seen around that time! But it's no joke, it's still vandalism all the same.'

'Can I speak to this restaurant owner?'

'No, sorry, unable to, data protection, you see. I cannot possibly reveal the name.'

'OK, well, thank you.' Edmund had drawn a blank.

'Just one other thing, though. If you are in that area, I would recommend the excellent Peking duck at The Lotus Flower in Gerrard Street. Cheers.' With that the council man hung up the telephone.

'May I speak please, with the owner?' Edmund asked the waiter.

'Owner is not there. Problem, sir?'

'No, no problem. I just would like to speak to the owner, not about the food, something else.'

Edmund felt he had better have an actual meal when he visited. So he sampled the early-evening special.

As he had walked past Gerrard Street earlier it had surprised him how much Peking duck was on display. In every window, each restaurant. People everywhere, vegetables being sold out of old carts. Tourists reading menus with hesitation, some committing to a place but others not and moving on.

The restaurant he wanted was in fact off the main street and set in a side street. A door of the building was still on Gerrard Street but seemed unused. The restaurant was small, bustling with activity, and immaculately clean and welcoming. The duck was very good indeed. Time had passed since his request to the waiter and Edmund was about to leave when a young woman appeared. She gave out an aura of authority as she came over to his table and asked why he wanted to see her. Edmund felt suddenly awkward and stood up. She was elegantly dressed and had a cut-glass accent. After some initial exchanges, she seemed happy to co-operate with his questioning.

'Why are you so interested in the sign?' she asked. They were still standing.

'I am researching the history of the area. Having strange occurrences like this adds, well, a little spice to the make-up of the place.' He thought this would do for now and he moved back towards his table.

She asked if they could move outside. There she slowly lit a cigarette and blew smoke into the air with a slight tilt of the head. She then gazed at him with a curious look. Her voice was much quieter now.

'If you really want to know, then I shall tell. It was the sign of a call to arms. At least in old Chinese mythology. I studied the particular era that it came from at Oxford, you see. Most people wouldn't notice the change in the sign. I have seen translations and signs change here before, but this was significant.'

'Why?' asked Edmund.

'It means "May Storm", in a strictly literal sense. But they are the first characters of a saga about the end of the world, if you believe that sort of thing. Certainly nothing to do with Wardour Street and a world away from the City of Westminster.'

Edmund was even more curious. He filled in some facts. 'My friend was looking at it, I think it definitely meant something to him.' He was changing his story.

She looked surprised and asked. 'So, who is your friend?'

After a long silence Edmund clapped his hands. 'Well, I must be going now. I have taken up your time. One last thing, could I ask what actually happens in the story, the saga as you call it.' They both walked together back to the doorway again.

'Well . . .' she smiled standing in the door frame. 'It is about a brave warrior who for the sake of his own people fights alone against their enemy. The enemy is a dragon-like beast, allegorical of course and symbolic of all our worst fears.'

Something resonated within Edmund's head and he paused. 'Look, can you do one last thing, can you show me the symbols?'

'Well, I can write them for you if you like.'

They walked back inside and she pulled at a note pad. With slow and elegant movements of her hand she created three characters on the pad. Edmund had seen them many years ago, it was the tattoo on Stewart's left wrist.

Edmund's father was a retired naval officer. He lived alone, save for a housekeeper, some twenty minutes away from the town. Edmund would visit normally around fortnightly, but he wanted to see him now. As a Royal Navy Commander, his father had served on many tours in South East Asia. He witnessed the end of the British Empire and his voyages had taken him to Malaysia and Singapore, and also to China, of which Hong Kong was an outpost he spoke of a lot. He had commanded HMS *Hermes* in Hong Kong harbour at the time of an incident with Communist activists in Hong Kong during the 1960s. He was sure that the phrase 'May Storm' was something his father had mentioned to him, or at least that he may know something about it. Certainly his old Dad loved talking about his time in the Royal Navy so it would be not a wasted exercise if it came to nothing.

Edmund drove to his father's bungalow set in a semi-circular ordinary-looking road. It was on the edge of an estate which was notable for its varied plantation of trees, at this time of year verdant and full. They would never plant like this in new estates, his Dad would often say. Edmund had parked his car in the drive and saw his father's face at the window. He was standing upright, looking out. He liked to see what was going on and rarely missed any domestic happening in the estate if it involved the road. Each car's destination could be accurately traced to each house on the estate. New vehicles were observed with interest, the time of arrival logged in his head.

'What do you want, son?' his father asked.

'Look, Dad, I don't come to see you just because I want something!'

'Well, you are not due to visit until Sunday.' Edmund gave his father a huge bear hug. His father looked slightly uncomfortable when he did so.

'Come in then. Tea?'

His father nodded to his housekeeper. She was Singaporean and his father described her as a refugee. This always amused Edmund. She was relatively young and exceptionally good-looking.

The walls of the front room were decorated with Far East memorabilia. On the writing desk by the bay window was a prized possession, an official photograph of Edmund's father's investiture ceremony, when he received a CBE from the Queen on his retirement. He looked so very young even then. Edmund studied his father's considerably older face and sat down. He explained that he wanted to pick his brains on a Chinese puzzle. His father was immediately engaged.

'What kind of puzzle?'

'What some characters mean to you exactly.'

'Well!' He looked disappointed. 'That's not a puzzle, it's a translation.'

'I just wanted to see what you thought.' Edmund handed over the Gerrard Street paper note with the characters written on it. Edmund added some background.

'The characters I am told mean "May Storm". I am sure you have used this phrase before when you have told me about your time in Hong Kong, but I can't remember in what context.'

His father reached for his reading glasses and presented them to his face slowly. At that point tea for two on a large tray was being brought into the room rather noisily. His father waited for the housekeeper to leave and reverently placed the note in front of him. There was a moment's pause, then: 'Oh yes, May Storm all right!' He looked suddenly grave.

'You have told me about this, perhaps a story from China?' His father looked up at him.

'You have a very good memory. Yes, I would have spoken about it, particularly to your late mother. This was the name given to an incident but at that time there were many details I couldn't divulge even to you.'

Edmund asked, 'Do you mean secret?'

'Yes, it was classified as Most Secret. These words are, well certainly were, very dangerous cryptology. At least it was considered so many decades ago.' His father began to relate the story of his time in Hong Kong.

Edmund noticed that his father was now totally engaged in the subject, recounting facts with fast expressive tones, including the fact that HMS *Hermes* under his command was stationed in Hong Kong Harbour in 1967. It was a time of extreme tension between the Hong Kong colony and mainland China. Continual industrial action and protests by Communist-led unions had led to serious rioting in the streets and general disorder involving substantial loss of life. Her Majesty's Government were concerned that China might use the general unrest as an excuse to cross the border, essentially to invade Hong Kong. The British Embassy in Peking had been burnt down by Red Guards and the resident consul (there was no ambassador recognised then by Communist China) had fled. The local Hong Kong Communist leaders were well organised and well funded. They met in secret and after dark. Hong Kong had an emergency declared by the then Governor and a strict night-time curfew enforced. It was a top priority that any such activities or meetings of such leaders were monitored.

It was the middle of July 1967 and British intelligence had, through the resident office of GCHQ in Hong Kong, discovered what they believed was the Communists' call sign to the Chinese to invade. This sign would be communicated by radio at the time of maximum social disorder, so that China could claim that it was in fact she that was a liberator, bringing order and freedom. The old naval man continued on the theme of order and freedom:

'*Order?* Well, the People's Liberation Army – the PLA – would certainly bring in substantial numbers of well-trained troops and there would be order all right, my God! *Freedom?* Well, poor fools, they had no idea of the carnage that would ensue from invasion. We could only evacuate about 2000 people maximum from the Colony, even with six to twelve hours' notice. It was a doomsday scenario!' He paused and looked out of the window. Rain was starting to tap on the glass. He looked out for some time, gathering thoughts before continuing:

'This, my dear boy is that very call sign. If it was transmitted that would have been the end of the Colony as we knew it.' He held the paper up dramatically. 'It literally means May Storm.'

Edmund looked at the floppy piece of paper which had such significance in his past, then back to his father. 'Would they really have come in just on that signal?'

His father nodded. 'We had been well briefed on the fact that battalions of the PLA where positioned not that far from the border in Yantian Province. The local activists were well organised and we had Intel . . . we had intelligence, that the AB Communist Group could summon them with this call sign. They used to meet in old office blocks after curfew.'

'AB Group?' asked Edmund.

'Sorry, that was the acronym for the Anti-British Communist People's Struggle Group, to give it its full title. It was supported by the Peking government, both politically and financially. Highly organised and efficient, money would come through via Guangzhou as I recall.'

His father strode around his front room, waving his arms to give flavour as if addressing a de-briefing session. He continued, 'The Royal Navy was brought in in the form of HMS *Hermes* and HMS *Bulwark* as a sign of our resolve. I had been diverted in *Hermes* from Singapore.'

He carried on, 'We knew they had an organising executive committee, or so they called it, known as The Twelve. And we knew they would meet regularly after the curfew set under the Emergency Regulations. Only we didn't know exactly where they would meet. If we caught them in a meeting then this itself was an offence in Hong Kong at that time. A meeting not authorised by the HK Government consisting of three people or more was an illegal assembly in May to September 1967. The Secret Intelligence Service had paid agents and informants on the ground – hawkers, traders, doormen and the like. They were our eyes!'

He was on a roll now, recalling events decades ago as if it happened last week. But his father would forget things that actually happened last week.

'We would try and intercept meetings but somehow they would get wind of it and disappear. Then out of the blue an agent revealed the next intended location of a meeting of The Twelve. But it was tight, as we needed to act within thirty minutes in order to apprehend them. It was an office building in North

Point, so on Hong Kong Island, right under our nose. On the signal from Joint Command I gave the order to scramble five Wessex helicopters from my ship's main deck. Each had Hong Kong Police Tactical Unit men, Gurkhas and chaps from the Special Boat Squadron.'

Edmund knew 'my ship' meant HMS *Hermes*. His father's eyes were glinting with pride and he didn't want to stop him.

'To get them all together was critical. That very day was the worst day of riotous unrest. The 'copters arrived at the top of the office block and our chaps abseiled down on to its roof in about four minutes flat. Total surprise. We caught the whole lot plus the comms equipment, which we took before they could signal.'

Edmund's father sat down now. He let out a long blow of breath. 'Those were heady days, that's for sure. But what I remember most.' His voice fell much quieter now. 'I was responsible for the detention on board of The Twelve. The orders were to keep them off land until our key intelligent agents were pulled off the ground.'

Edmund was curious why he had never heard of this. 'You had all of the so-called Twelve on your own ship? Did you meet with them?'

'Of course. It was my duty to explain that they were under the command and authority of Her Majesty's Navy and that Hong Kong Emergency Regulations meant we could lawfully detain them without limit of time, as they were a risk to the security of the Colony.'

'And how did they react to that?'

'Well, what I remember, I can remember it well even after all these years, was that they were not irrational maniacs or anything like that. Certainly not motivated by money – we tried that tactic! They sincerely believed that they were campaigning to offer the ordinary people of the Colony a better future. They revealed nothing of any use to us. They were as calm as anything. After some time they were moved from the ship to the Mount Street Detention Centre to be further interrogated. I communicated this order in person to their leader, a local chap by the name of Lee. Yes, that's it.'

At this point Edmund had to make way as his father walked past him to go to another room in the house. He returned some minutes later with what looked like a logbook or diary.

With an earnest expression on his face, his father looked look through the pages, and with a grunt he found the salient log entry:

24 August 1967
Order received for Abercrombies to be removed to Mount Street by 0100 hours.

Informed Lee (26793) as leader of the prisoners. Same showed no emotion as throughout – was educated and thoughtful. Courtesy in his dealing with authority. Too bright to be involved in needless reactionary tactics in custody. Told me that he had all the time the world could give (his words) hence his further detention of no consequence to the so called struggle. Looked me in the eye and said the future of Hong

Kong shall be within China and that it was an unrelenting force against which we had no shield. Reported said comment to Admiralty.

The logbook, as if a piece of treasure, was placed down carefully.

'I had forgotten our nickname for the AB commies group. It was the *Abercrombies*.'

'What did Admiralty say about the comment?'

'Never heard anything. I thought it might . . .' His father laughed. 'I thought it might be treasonable or some such thing. But the fact was the fella was right! Almost exactly 30 years later the handover to China took place – 1997 and all that. It was peaceful, mind, but we handed it back to them like he predicted.'

'What happened to them?'

'The Twelve, you mean?'

'Yes, and the ring leader.'

'They were detained for a long time and, rather shamefully, never put on trial. I was ordered to proceed with a voyage to Singapore some weeks later. By that time the riots in Hong Kong were calming down and order was restored. I never heard what became of Lee. As I said, the interrogations never revealed anything of use. It was the fact that all The Twelve were picked up in one hit that was decisive. The way the building was stormed by us resonated around South East Asia.'

Edmund intervened. 'You always told me the Chinese admired strength, not weakness!'

'Quite so, quite so! What it did was show we were committed

to the Colony. Changes were made of course afterwards – improved hours and employment rights for workers and such like. But it could not hide the unfortunate truth that fifty-one people died in Hong Kong in the 1967 riots. Over four thousand people arrested and detained.'

His father wanted to go back to the characters on the paper, the call sign: 'Now how did you come by them?'

Edmund explained about his friend's death, his tattoo and the sign at Wardour Street.

'The thing is, what would Stewart be doing with these characters on his arm?'

His father looked concerned. 'Well it's either a total coincidence or it's associated in some way with that period of history. If anyone was caught with those characters on their person in those days, he would have been in trouble. Had he ever been to Hong Kong?'

'He worked there, I think for the Foreign Office, it would have been around the time of the handover.

'Did he work in Intelligence?'

'Possibly. There is some rumour that he did.'

'What is his surname?'

'Kilbride.'

His father grunted again. 'Hmm, I don't recognise the name. You need to report the fact that these have reappeared. It may mean something. I can speak to people I know.'

'Hang on for a little bit if you could. Look, he is dead now. What good could it do?'

* * *

Edmund left later that evening when it had turned dark, the rain falling harder against his car window. He now had to contemplate betraying his dead friend's secret. He waved to his father, who was there standing at the window as if on the bridge of a warship. Edmund would need to look further into Stewart's background. But where would he start? The only place to start would be Angie. She may know more about his Hong Kong days.

When Edmund had turned the corner into the main road his father reached for the telephone.

6. OLIVER

The carpet shop that Oliver Parker owned and managed was not in an ideal location. There was no parking in this area and it was the wrong side of the town. Carpets were not what people seemed to want and some time ago Oliver extended the shop range to wood flooring. This was not a huge success. The wood flooring section was now just a corner over by the water dispenser and stainless-steel coffee-maker. The rest of the shop was a maze of assorted designs, samples and fabrics. And carpets everywhere. Every part of the shop was taken up with merchandise. The main checkout area was surrounded by sample books. Stacked up high, they looked precarious, as if they would fall. There were plenty of carpet displays and loads of samples, but the same could not be said about customers.

'What time we finish today?' asked Lina. This was a sign that the shop footfall had been particularly low. Oliver usually closed early if no customers appeared after lunch.

'I have got to get on with the VAT return, so let's close at four-thirty, shall we?'

He was not sure why he left it as a question, but he relied on Lina to hold the fort on Saturdays. Staff were difficult to get hold of.

'Yes, OK. I prepare now. Hey, the mad cow is coming in!'

The door opened and in stepped an older lady. It was Mrs Fergus, sporting a fine head of grey hair and dressed in her favourite tartan skirt. She enthusiastically acknowledged Oliver.

'Oh, Mr Parker, there you are! You well, I trust?'

'Ahhh, Mrs Fergus. How the devil are you?'

'Mr Parker, I knew that you would be pleased to see me!' He wasn't.

'How can I help you today?' he asked, emphasising the word *you*.

Mrs Fergus normally passed her time in the shop as though an enthusiastic visitor at a museum. She had a section of carpets that she liked to visit regularly. Oliver was sure that once she had actually bought something in the shop but it was some years back. Lina had no experience of that. Relations between them were usually tense.

'We close this shop!' Lina said suddenly with her Georgian (normally mistaken for Russian) accented English. It was more noticeable when she was angry.

'Oh, my dear, don't mind me. If you ask me . . .' She looked outside. 'This area isn't safe. Much better in here, you know.' Lina gave Oliver a withering look.

'You never know what might happen. At my age, they want your savings!' Mrs Fergus looked very sternly at Oliver, before smiling again. 'I wouldn't want to trouble you with that, would I, Mr Parker?' Oliver shook his head gravely.

'I mean all the strange goings-on, you know, around here,' she carried on. Oliver decided to pretend to be busy stacking carpet samples.

'You know, only this morning I saw none other than Stewart Kilbride! Clear as day down in Green Lane.'

Lina felt she needed to chip in at this point. 'He dead, Stewart is dead – what is matter with you? You crazy?'

'Well, dear, I know. I was very surprised when I saw him but it were him all right!'

'Mrs Fergus, is there anything that I can help you with? Lina is correct. Poor Stewart has passed away.'

It was some time later before Oliver was able to leave the shop. With the prospect of ghost figures appearing in the town, his assistant Lina had promptly left the shop. Mrs Fergus agreed to be driven home by him. Stewart was not coming back to life, he assured her. Perhaps she is mad after all, he thought.

'This is the one!' Mrs Fergus suddenly shouted. A commuter on his way home from the station was startled with the abrupt braking. They were outside her cottage. He bade her farewell. 'Would you like some gooseberry fool to take home?' she asked.

Oliver had bad memories of this particular dessert when he last took it home from Mrs Fergus' cottage. The boys, who were at home then, were badly sick and Oliver and his wife Sam had intense stomach pain. Only Nicola was spared. He said no and left.

The drive back to his home led to the top of Graysmere. He stopped and looked out. From there you could see the fold of the Downs. It was lit up by the glow of warm evening summer light that only the English countryside seems to produce. The air had a sensual feel about it, as though one could reach and touch it. Down below was the green, where the youngsters were playing. The evening was so still that they could easily be heard high up, where Oliver was now stopped.

Oliver opened the back door to the house. Sam was feeding Nicola in her chair. This chair was automated, which had made a huge difference. Although no voice or even emotion was expressed, he could see it in her eyes. Often they were dark and brooding. Now they seemed to be brighter. Just little things which meant so much.

'How was your day?' said Sam to her husband, not looking up. It had to be answered carefully. It had been a boring day for him but then Sam was a full-time carer for their seriously disabled teenage daughter. Committed and total care. Oliver was ashamed to think that he was probably not capable himself of carrying out these tasks, all day and every day.

'Not many in the shop today, but I was able to get the VAT done. We took a load more this time last year. I don't understand it.' He sat down. 'How are you, Nicola?'

There was no answer. He smiled and reached out to touch her hand. The contact was brief and was precious. Sam looked troubled and it was later that evening when they were alone together in the sitting room that Sam told him, 'Doctor Ridgeway says there has been significant decline in Nicola's condition. It breaks my heart to have to be told this.' Tears welled up in her eyes and fell down her cheek. 'There is so much bad news at the moment; your friend from the Club dead, Jamie unhappy at school. But what has Nicola done to deserve this? She seemed to have accepted the chair so well.'

'How much . . . how long did he say, for Nicola?'

'A gradual deterioration for the next three to six months. Reduced life expectancy.'

'Oh my God, look we can deal with this.'

She looked up at him. 'For goodness' sake don't preach at me and don't, don't say you will be saying prayers for her – I can't take any of that now.'

'It's what I believe, I wouldn't say it if I didn't think it important. I believe it can help.'

Sam sobbed and took a tissue from the box by the fruit bowl. 'Well, it doesn't seem to be helping, nope, that's for sure, it isn't helping.'

'We must try to be positive . . .'

Sam interrupted and stood up. 'Positive? And you think I am fucking not then? How do you think I feel each morning when I have to make the most of her wretched day, for her sake, and for us as well, as a family?' Sam paused, staring out to the garden. 'I make every day matter for her, she is still with us. Your friend, I am sorry to say and it's sad, but he is not with us any more. Life is for us living. I will give Nicola

71

the best life with or without prayers and rosary beads.'

Sam stood up and reached for the mantelpiece. 'We have had another letter from Jamie.' Sam was changing the subject.

'How is he?'

'You better read it.'

The paper was school headed notepaper and the letter was written in Jamie's own hand, in fountain pen and ink. It was a school rule to write thus, biros and similar items were considered inferior. As Oliver read it, he could see marks like little drawings of clouds where Jamie's tears had fallen and smeared the ink. After some time he put the letter down.

'Why don't they do something about it, the teachers, that is?' said Oliver, breaking the silence.

'Do they know the problem? We have said there were issues with certain boys, but it was rather laughed off, if I remember rightly. You are going to have to speak with the Head again.'

'He is clearly not happy, maybe . . .'

'Maybe what?'

'Time to take him out?'

Sam looked cross. 'Well, now you are changing your tune. You totally dismissed this idea when I mentioned this before, and now he has exams coming up.'

'Well, with Stewart dead I am thinking differently about things.'

'How does that make me feel? So I don't matter then?'

'You know that's not true, it's that I realise how important all our time is. Stewart's girlfriend, you know, Angie, is pregnant with his child. He is never going to see it, the child that is. I want to make the best of my time with Jamie. He is coming home.'

Oliver drove to the school. It was decided not to make a big thing of it. Some of the boys didn't know he was being taken out of school. Oliver parked by the school chapel and met Jamie there. 'Hi, Dad.' There was no hug, not in front of the whole school.

'I have got to see the Bursar, you could wait here.'

'Fine, how long will you be?'

'Not long at all. I just have to take a cheque and sign something.'

Oliver walked through the main door into the corridor that led to the great hall. There was a smell of food and the sound of clattering from the kitchens. The route to the Bursar's office took him past scores of sporting photographs of First Elevens or First Fifteens. One such photo caught his eye, it was dated 5 July 1912. There was a formal-looking games master among eleven boys of 17 or 18. Enthusiastic-looking fresh faces in abundance. Two years before the start of the Great War. He pondered how many of this team served their country and lived to play the game again. In fact, every face in that corridor could tell its own story. Oliver eventually reached the Bursar's office.

'And finally would your son like to join the old boys' association?' asked the Bursar after the business was dealt with. 'For a modest annual payment you get a magazine and can keep in touch with the school.'

Oliver was taken aback. 'Well, I must say that just about sums up this place. You have taken our money for the last two years, our son has been unhappy and you have done nothing about it. So now we are taking him out and having still to pay a whole term's fees. You seriously think he wants to join this association or whatever it is.'

'Oh, I see.' The Bursar, Oliver couldn't remember her name, looked perplexed. 'It is just that nearly all the boys join on leaving . . .'

'Well, James Parker is not one of them.' Oliver left without saying any more. He thought it probably rude to not say goodbye in retrospect, but then it risked trying to remember the person's name. Now Oliver felt strangely triumphant walking back to the car. Jamie was outside the car with a group of boys, looking shy.

'Are we all ready to go?'

'The guys have got me a present, for leaving.'

Oliver smiled at the three boys. In spite of the hateful perse-cution of his son by others at this school, here were some true friends. What looked like books, chewing gum and vouchers were handed over.

'You must write and tell us what it is like to have girls in your class!' the tallest one said to Jamie. They shook hands in a formal way, with a gentle tap on the other's shoulder. The car drove away, the friends busy waving and punching each other in jest. He never did see them again.

The drive home was silent for the start of the journey. Jamie seemed to be taking in this change of circumstance. Later he asked about his new school, plans for the summer, and if Nicola was OK.

'I shall be able to spend loads of time with her now. That was one of the problems in the term, I had to go and leave her. I can't wait to see her.'

Oliver knew that he had promised not to reveal her life expectancy to Jamie but the fact he was now home would mean this may have to change. But that was for another day.

'Mum wrote to say a team mate of yours had died suddenly?'

'Yes, it was very sad, we are all very upset. We are going to have an end-of-season dinner in his honour. Maybe one of the trophies can be named after him.'

'Was his name Stewart?'

'Yes, that is a good memory.'

'I remember him at that charity father-and-son match last year. He was a reserve for one of the boys who didn't have a dad.'

'Guy?'

'Yeah, and he said he was a top bloke. He said he never properly knew his own father and to step in was a real privilege. Guy asked him what happened to his Dad.'

'What, you are joking me?'

'What is wrong with that? He answered the question.'

Oliver confessed that there was nothing impolite in the question if Stewart had opened up conversation in this way. It was odd though, as Oliver knew Stewart was a very private person.

'*Taken from me, interned if you like.* That's what he said to Guy. Like he was a prisoner of some kind.' Jamie looked at his Dad. 'But I've got you.' At once Jamie looked embarrassed.

'I suppose you felt a prisoner at school!' It was meant as a light-hearted way of continuing the conversation. Jamie had other ideas.

'It's worse than prison. You are innocent, haven't done anything to deserve it, and then you have to deal with that hell.'

'Look, it's done now, we are going home. Mum's cooking tonight.'

They passed by unfamiliar fields and roads until after a while Jamie recognised the location.

'It's great to be going home, though. I used to feel sad when we drove through this tunnel, as if it was taking me to another world.'

They passed under a large railway embankment through a tunnel substantially longer than one would associate with the area. It was dark inside and, strangely, on entering you couldn't see light at the other end. The nature of the terrain did look different once through on the other side.

'Like the Bridge of Sighs in Venice perhaps?'

'Well that did connect to a prison, I guess!'

Oliver could tell his son was gradually becoming more cheerful.

'I won't miss it, but I shall miss my mates.'

'You will have new ones before you know it.'

'They may already have a circle of friends.'

'At your age you always make friends.'

Oliver wasn't himself convinced by this observation. It was something he had always found difficult when younger.

When they arrived home the reaction from Nicola was immediate. Her head would move from side to side and she would gaze at Jamie. There was love in those eyes, any parent could see that. Jamie took her hand. In his own way, by looking at her he was communicating to her that he was not going away again. He tried to wipe the tears. That school was not for him, he had a fresh start ahead. Someone else could have his place at school. Hopefully they could make the most of it all. Maybe they would be better suited to the task. Hsarretchester School was not for him.

7. FAROKH

The air was heavy with heat and dust. They had all walked long enough now with their suitcases but the driver still could not be found. Maybe he had the wrong street. They sat under a jujube tree to escape the worst of the sun. The traders in the local market stalls were hard at work competing with shouts of best deals as if in a contest. Small drops of perspiration fell off Farokh's face and made little dark marks in the ground. He put his travel case down. Farokh, his mother, father and sister, all packed and ready to go. Then they noticed a large smart car appearing at the end of the road with a group of street kids running excitedly alongside it. Farokh's father told his family to get in, it had cool air inside. They then left behind sweat and noise with his father in the front seat speaking to the driver. At the first crossroads the car stopped and a spindled old man moved off the side of the road and stood in front of the car. His face was weathered and leathery. He held his hand up as if to bless them. Was he a holy man?

* * *

Farokh never forgot the face of the old man when he thought back to the day they left India. Also he never forgot that signal he made. Was it a warning like his father had always said it was afterwards?

That was a long time ago, but his father felt that the emigration to England was cursed. The job that his father had come to seek never materialised and it was only years later, with the job market improved, that he finally secured a living for his family. By then it was too late to return to India.

Farokh was named after his father's favourite wicket-keeper and cricket brought some solace to his life in England. Farokh excelled at school, went to university and also played the game! His father would burst with pride when Farokh visited him in the nursing home, and he wanted to hear stories of matches in the town.

For Farokh it meant mixing with people he never normally saw. Stewart was one of these. In fact, Stewart was one of the few people in the team who asked where Farokh had originated from. There was such sensitivity that Farokh felt that he must be an outsider. Although interested in Indian culture, Gujarati was beyond the reach of Stewart's considerable language skills. Stewart did know about being a Parsi and spoke often with him about it. In fact, Stewart tried to be a father figure to him. He himself had given him the nickname Faro which stuck with the others. Stewart had also met his father. Faro never thought it was that unusual a request, in fact it seemed normal to him. His father seemed pleased to have another visitor and one who was a guiding light to his son and who was British. Something he had yearned for himself.

Faro was now tasked with a drive to the nursing home in order to tell his father that Stewart was dead. It would upset him, he always asked after him every time he visited. He had to tell him.

The nursing home was once the country seat of a wealthy family. Set in considerable parkland grounds, the house was sold to pay off huge gambling debts that one member of the family had incurred. Faro parked in one of the available spaces and asked for his father at the main reception. Faro sat nearby and smiled at nurses who passed by, one of whom smiled back and enquired whether it was he, then led him through corridors to his father's room.

His father hugged his son tight and kissed his forehead. They spoke randomly, about matters that came into their heads.

'And what of Stewart?' asked his father cheerfully.

There was an awkward silence.

'*Dedi* – I had meant to tell you, but he is dead, Stewart was found dead.'

'Oh . . . Oh my.' He looked up at the ceiling, then looked down again, trying to conceal tears. It made Faro desperately sad to see him like this. After a period of silence his father spoke again.

'He was someone that would look after you, guide you here in the ways of this country.'

'I know, *Dedi*, it is very sad but I can look after myself and I have you.'

'No, you cannot see it as I do, or Stewart did. You see, he wrote me a letter.'

'A letter? From Stewart, you didn't tell me!'

'It only arrived last week. I was going to talk about it on your next visit. So I shall talk about it now.'

'What did he write about?'

Faro's father handed him a letter. It was typed on sturdy good-quality paper, with an opening greeting written by hand in black ink. Faro started to read the contents. After initial pleasantries expressed to his father it read:

I have always enjoyed our discussions, particularly on the topic of Colonial rule. I felt this was a subject you knew well. Your views are not tainted by the grandiose vision of glorious empire, but rather the naked truth. The suppression of the individual, the scant regard to culture or religions that have lasted thousands of years. In brief, the subjugation of the people. You yourself were disillusioned at home, hence your journey to the so-called mother country, leaving all behind. How I wish I could have been there to stop you!

My life has been to contemplate damage done. In my own particular case, damage to my own father, imprisoned by the British in China; or as it was at the time, rented from China. My mother was left to fend for herself and to offer up to me as much of parenthood as she could muster. I never knew my father in the way that Farokh knows you. He is a fine boy and you must make sure he is always in touch with you.

For my part, I will not be able to visit again. I regret this but I am responding to the call from my own nation. It is the place of my birth and it belongs to me. The People's Republic never forgot my father and I have tried in my own way to return to them that same hope he had with him when alone.

So I say farewell and ask that you please keep this letter completely private other than from Faro, who I trust.

Never give in to them. Again I ask: Say nothing about this letter or anything that has happened between us.

With kind wishes,
Stewart Kilbride

Faro placed the letter down and looked up. 'So, is he saying that he is Chinese?'

'Yes, he told me that his father was from China, his mother was from Scotland and worked as a nanny in Hong Kong. When his father was imprisoned, she had to bring him up on her own, as British. But he must have wanted to do something for China and for his late father, I suppose.'

'*Dedi* – we must contact the police.'

'Hah, there speaks an English boy!'

'From what it says here he may not be dead after all. That is what I mean, we must tell the authorities, this is wrong.'

'We leave him damn well alone. It is what he wants for the honour of his family. I salute him!'

'No, *Dedi*. Look, if not the police we must tell somebody.'

'He trusted me with it . . .' The letter was held in the air and he continued, '. . . and he trusted you. May I be struck down by all the Gods if I was to breach his trust in me.'

Faro looked at his father, his eyes were defiant. He then thought of Stewart. So much the perfect British gentleman but always so disdainful of authority. There were so many places in the world that he spoke about. Maybe he knew so many places that he never had a feeling of home. Always on the move and never settled. Faro's mind wandered to his first meeting with Stewart Kilbride.

It was cold, dry but cold at the start of a season. End of April or early May. They had both arrived early at the opposition ground for an away match. Nothing seemed open, no obvious signs of activity. Faro had tried a door and a man approached and barked at him 'What you doing, boy? There's nothing there that will interest you.' He wore an ironic smile. As an overweight figure, he looked like an aged wrestler longing for a last bout.

'You work here?' Stewart said, walking into view from behind a pillar. The wrestler looked surprised that Faro had company.

'Yes, and we are not opened up yet.'

'Well, my good man, I suggest you open up now, or have you got some hovel you call an office that you can disappear to?' The smile evaporated. Stewart continued: 'Well, are you going to open up? You know how to do it, I hope?' The recipient of this question chose not to reply but they were soon in the changing rooms.

It was then that Stewart spoke with Faro. It was on the subject of never letting *them* speak to you in that manner. Strength was the only thing that was respected, show no weakness. It was the reference to *them* that was so curious to Faro at the time. And why would he be so concerned about something that Faro saw regularly? It was of no obvious concern to Stewart – he told him so. Stewart had then said we can all do something about it, in our own way, like sand passing through a glass dial. Only fractions of pieces but over enough time they come together and cannot be stopped.

Faro was now back in the present with his father and the letter. He pondered about the use of that particular word, never give in to *them*, it said. He asked his father about the final part of the letter and his father read it out again.

Say nothing about this letter or anything that has happened.

'*Dedi*, what does it mean when he says "anything that has happened"?'

His father looked at him. I ask my boy to keep my confidence so I must tell him everything. 'Have you ever wondered who pays for this place?' His father swept his arm around as if tracing a half-circle.

Faro responded, 'When you had to take your early retirement due to ill health, this was part of the arrangement from the rail company or its insurers, it is all paid for.'

'It is paid for, that is correct, but not by them bastards! No, it was Stewart, he said to me that he would get the money from somewhere and he did.'

'But why did you not tell us this?'

'Part of it was the shame of it. If I couldn't be cared for here by these wonderful angels, it would have been a burden on my family. Also, because he is in the team. I didn't want any embarrassment whenever you saw him.'

'We are talking many thousands, *Dedi*, that is a huge sum for one person to raise.'

'I know but he wanted to do this for me, he was a compassionate man. Secret man, but he had a heart like an Indian Tiger, my boy. He didn't like the British, I could tell that. He gave the money unconditionally to me.'

It was hard to take in for Faro, too much to consider. Should this money now be repaid? If so, to whom – did Stewart have any dependents? Faro felt that he needed to leave and to contemplate.

'Look I have to think about this. I shall come back.'

'Yes, but come back soon, we can talk about it some more together.'

Faro kissed his father and then left the room, passing down the corridor. Before turning to the main entrance hall, he looked back to see his father at the door of his room. He was holding his index finger to his mouth. It looked almost mystical. How his father would like that, Faro thought to himself. Was Stewart's gesture considered by his father to be the end of the original curse?

During his drive home Faro tried to contemplate what all this must mean to his father. He thought he had understood how his father felt and what motivated him. Faro saw his own Britain differently. There were times when he felt like an outsider here, particularly in this part of the country, in fact. But Faro was able to make money, good money. He was not going to let negative views on his adopted country get in the way of that. Why should he have this on his conscience – handed out charity without any consultation with the family? Faro cared not for Stewart's own fatherly admiration of him – not if it could affect his own future success. He wanted to be a *Voriyara*! One who has and will succeed in this country. He would not need help and would do so on his own terms, Farokh was certain of that.

8. GEORGE

George was the youngest in the team. He had the task on a match day of running to the pavilion in order to switch on the industrial-sized kitchen water heater to prepare for tea. This had to be carried out at a precise time – around 30 minutes before the sandwiches and cakes were dropped off. This in turn was 45 minutes before the two sides stopped for the tea break. Experiments had been carried out with timers. Also, the water heater had in previous fixtures been turned on low at the start of the match. However, both of these attempts had failed and also led to a series of unfortunate explosions, with the loss of the usual tea-maker volunteer to a stress-related condition. George was tasked with this job as no one else could be bothered. Also, he was playing his first match after finishing term at school. To George it was an introduction to acceptance in an adult world. A sense of trust in him. He carried out the task enthusiastically, then ran back on to the pitch.

It was the skipper who told him what to do but also he took advice from Stewart. Those two ran things on the pitch, a captain with his right-hand man. George liked Stewart and sensed that he always seemed to be the one in control. But George was sure he saw him smoking dope after the match. Well it smelt like it – what a lad! He never did tell Mum because she wouldn't approve. Everything was fine as long as George got home safe. This was never tested to the full. If Stewart's driving skills or another of the team were erratic following a match, he would ask that they drop him around the corner first. This would ensure that they wouldn't be asked in – how awkward that would be! But this time Stewart was quiet in the car and seemed engrossed in something.

George remembered back to the day of the first car journey home from a match with Stewart driving. He recalled Stewart talking in the car to Tomas about life in Hong Kong. Did they play the game there?

'Oh yes, very much so. I played a lot in Hong Kong. It was a good way to meet people, get to know them. Standard was high.'

'How long were you in Hong Kong?' George asked.

'I lived there when young, and I also went to work there after graduating. You hoping to go to University?'

'No, I would never get the grades! Anyway people at my school don't go there. Where did you go?'

'Hsarretchester and Oxford.'

'Both?' George smiled.

'Sure, one was school and one was University.'

'Wow. So Hsarretchester is the school!'

'Yes, I think that is right, it is the school as far as I am concerned.'

'It is not for my type.' At this Stewart had looked puzzled.

'What do you mean? Education is for everyone.'

George shook his head. 'You need money and we don't have it at home.'

'They do scholarships for the sixth form. They encourage people to apply, and they also look for keen sportspeople. You play for the county, right?'

'Yes, and the South East region.'

'Well, there you are then, they would love to see you.'

'I don't know what my Mum would say, anyway not since Dad died.'

'I am sorry to hear that.'

'If it's one of them posh schools, my Mum wouldn't let me anyway, as Dad would turn in his grave.'

'I could speak to her, about the scholarships, that is. You would love the facilities there, everything about it in fact. Let me speak to her about it . . . could be my legacy.'

'What?'

'Nothing, just thinking about the route to your house.'

'You were just about to say something about a legacy!'

'Was I? This is your place, isn't it?'

It was that word 'legacy' that George remembered most. He recalled that moment and that word after he heard that Stewart had died. George wondered whether he knew he was going to die and was trying to help him in some way. Certainly his offer was too good to ignore.

Stewart even went so far as to sit down with George's mother to persuade her to agree to George applying for a sports scholarship. This did the trick and George was accepted. A space had recently become available in the sixth form after a pupil had given notice that he wanted to leave. What George and his mother never knew was that the scholarship was not in fact an award of all the fees, but just a small proportion. Stewart asked the school that he donate in full the total balance of the fees for the whole two years, provided it was kept confidential.

As it turned out, the terms of the confidentiality clause were such that the secret ceased upon Stewart's death. The school informed George's mother by post shortly after the funeral. It was a huge shock to her and she felt guilty.

'Your Dad would have hated the charity of it all. He had pride, you see.'

'But it meant so much to Stewart.'

'It's your Dad, God bless his soul, that I care about!'

'But Mum, would Dad really have objected? I think he would have said to take the opportunity if it was there and use it for good. You know what he felt about education. It is possible to achieve anything and everything!'

His mother looked upset at the recital of words that her late husband used to speak. 'You are like a mini-him, you know, my love.'

George went on, 'Stewart seemed to know what was about to happen. I have got to make the most of it for his sake and Dad's, don't you think?'

'Your father was a union man through and through. He would have objected to that sort of school. I was able to accept a scholarship but not charity.'

It was this discussion with his mother which led George to discover more about his own father. It was something he had not to date undertaken himself. He always relied on his mother's tender recollections. She welcomed his desire to search further. After all, he was now old enough to learn for himself.

'His Union was his life, so start with that. He was high up in the organisation and should feature in the records,' she would say.

George began his quest by visiting the Amalgamated Transport and Municipal Workers Union headquarters library and archive. He had arranged to see the archivist at the Union offices in Stoke-on-Trent. It would be George who would then decide whether his father's strong Union belief and morals would tolerate this arrangement with the school. His mother had agreed that she had no objection to George's search of the past in this way.

George arrived at Stoke railway station in the afternoon summer sun. It was quiet, almost sleepy. As it was the middle of the afternoon, office workers were neither at lunch nor had left home for the day. Opposite the station was a very grand railway hotel, elegantly crafted for passengers of another time altogether. Now it looked a little out of place in its surroundings. A sign outside drew attention to the hotel's new spa facility.

After walking from the station and catching a convenient bus,

George arrived in the office district. Walking down the final turn to Epworth Street, he found the Union headquarters building and went inside. Once there he asked for the archivist. George sat waiting in the small reception area and admired the flags and banners which adorned the walls. The words *Strength in Union* featured heavily amongst representations of factories and, of course, steam locomotives. A poster on one of the walls was advertising the benefits of a stay at the Union holiday chalets at Croyd in Devon. The scene showed a family of four on the beach with a huge yellow sun in the background.

The archivist came down and asked for him a few minutes later. She seemed unlike how he imagined an archivist would look. Attractive-looking with feline features and short bobbed dark hair. He thought she looked young. In fact she was not much older than him. He thought she was very sexy and found himself staring at her. She also thought him young, very young.

'Well, you also look very different from those who normally search the archive here,' she replied to George's opening remark with a slight air of disdain. She then led the way upstairs to what looked like a library. The room itself was simply decorated. Books and records were held in plain wooden shelving, leather-bound copies in well-ordered rows. George was led to an opened selection of books and papers on a table.

'So I have looked up Derek Undercross, your father, and I have his records and details here. It goes back quite a way. He retired as Deputy Secretary General of the Union. I have set out the relevant papers for you.'

For the next two hours George looked at speeches his father had made and papers that he had written, as well as minutes of executive council meetings. Education did feature prominently, as well as his obvious dedication to public transport and its workers – his own trade, in fact. George saw evidence of accomplishments, grants and support for union members in difficulty, support for local schools, and holiday arrangements for retired members.

It was a great surprise when he read an entry concerning Hong Kong. It was an executive minute at a time that his father was considering a donation to be made to striking transport workers in Kowloon and on the Star Ferry line in the 1960s. It was a large donation, even by the standards of the time. The Union decided it must be kept secret, as the funds would assist in the event of a general strike and so would gain the attention of the Colonial Government. The Union had even discussed the matter with the British Transport Secretary at the time. She was a strong willed cabinet member and was an advocate of a policy of decolonisation. Unofficial approval was given to the proposal. An educational facility was to be established in the Colony to help children of striking workers and to provide medical help. This particular aim resonated with the Transport Secretary as her older sister was a campaigner for bringing education to those in need. The Union also had various links with workers' associations in the then former Empire: Singapore, Kuala Lumpur and the like. However this was very different. Here it was driven by a clear desire to improve the lot of ordinary working-class people through education, with direct help in setting up an infrastructure for teaching.

George left Stoke later that afternoon with a sense of pride in his father's ambitions. On this evidence, his father would not want George to turn down the chance of education at a prestigious school. He felt sure that despite its reputation of privilege his father would have wanted him to go. But also, here was a link to Hong Kong itself, this was where Stewart had lived at that very time, as Stewart had mentioned to him. George had copies made of various funding transactions and the contacts of the Union in Hong Kong. There was no mention of a Kilbride but there was one entry that intrigued him in the papers he had copied:

The remittance of funds for the crisis in Hong Kong to be made via the Guomindang Government in Guangzhou at Bank of China account . . . . [Redacted then deleted September 1972] Hong Kong. A member of The Twelve would give details of the account for final payment.

It was clear that his father's Union had given financial support in some way to workers in Hong Kong. It was described as a crisis. And some kind of British Government soundings had been taken by the union at the time.

He had enough to investigate further. The discovery of his father's life in the Union was not enough. There was now a possible link to Stewart. Was Stewart known to his father, and was that why Stewart was intervening in his life? George decided he needed to pursue it further. The answer to this was important to him, as he had never known much about his father. He would need to research. As with his school work, he would need to visit the county library and use the internet there. His mother's house had no such technology and in any event he wanted to keep it private from her.

The visit to the library took place the following week. It was an overtly grand Victorian building with a sweeping central staircase, rather like a train station. It was just off the centre in the county's largest market town, close to a Georgian square. He would come here at times for his homework and for emailing essays to school. George always used his mother's library card but he was now old enough to have his own library card. In order to use IT services, he was required to complete a brief registration procedure at the front reception desk. There sat a dull and flustered-looking librarian. He had a badge which bore the legend *I LOVE BOOKS*, with a large red heart on it.

The man asked George, 'What is the nature of your research on the County wireless *internet* facility?' There was emphasis on the word 'internet'.

What, why should I tell him? thought George, and said nothing.

'Excuse me, sir. I need to know for the computer,' said the man, pointing at his PC screen.

'The struggle for workers' rights in world industrial history,' George replied confidently.

The librarian looked satisfied with this, although no more cheerful, and sat down to type.

'Ed-u-ca-tion-al Re-search-ing.' The librarian spoke aloud as he was tapping the letters into his keyboard. 'That comes under the "Other" box on the system, and so I have to type in the reason myself!' He looked suddenly animated.

'Really?' said George.

'Yes, so here is the password.' A printed note was passed across. 'You get one hour free and then a charge will have to be paid per half hour. Printing from the net is extra. Here are our standard charges for printing services.' A typed sheet was then handed over. 'Enjoy!'

George noticed him watching as he walked to an available desk. Moving around a large bookshelf, he sat down at an available monitor. It was a quiet area, where nobody could disturb him. He looked up a search engine and put in 'The Wilson Government'. The internet moved into action and his quest had begun.

George already had the name of the Transport Secretary and using help gained from occasional trips back to the front desk, he was able to access a vast amount of information. Some of this had only recently become public information. George's first visit lasted three hours. He made at least four more visits and he was drawn into the excitement of reading Cabinet and other Government papers from the 1960s, made available under the thirty-year rule. Soon he had established enough information to be able to summarise it himself. He entered the information into a note book he had bought as follows:

The Amalgamated Transport and Municipal Workers' Union (the Union) make a substantial set of unconditional donations to local trades unions in Hong Kong, some of whom were not officially recognised by the HK government. The majority of payments were made during 1967, with the first being made in August 1966. The donations were declared by the Union as being for the furtherance of education and wellbeing of young people, which should be made available to all. The fact that payments were to be made out of the United Kingdom jurisdiction was sanctioned by a UK government minister who supported the Union. Exchange controls implemented by the Wilson government would ordinarily block such a financial transaction. The minister took no initial steps to put the matter before formal Cabinet or to suggest that the HK government were informed at the time. The matter was finally raised at Cabinet level in July 1967, when Hong Kong was discussed following a series of local civilian fatalities. The Prime Minister said that whilst he was sympathetic to the fate of Chinese (sic) workers, the British government had more important world issues to contend with due to the Arab–Israeli War that had broken out that month. There was then a comparison between the Middle East conflict, described as a crisis of worldwide magnitude, and the situation in Hong Kong which in Cabinet minutes was said to be 'a May Storm in Her Majesty's Governor's breakfast tea cup'. Information on the donations is difficult to find after this Cabinet meeting. This is consistent with Union records. No further funds were sent from the Union to Hong Kong after July 1967. It was clear therefore that funds were sent to Hong Kong by the Union with the full knowledge of the British government and despite the fact that open support for the Hong Kong strikers was not official policy. The recipient bank details were provided from Hong Kong by a member of a committee or organising group of sorts representing various trades unions (most of which were illegal). The group was known as The Twelve. The arrangements were kept highly confidential. The person's name was Lee, however nothing is known about this person.

So with this information George satisfied himself in two ways. First, he believed his father would have approved the scholarship proposal. All his instincts were that he would be fine about it. Secondly, his friend Stewart Kilbride was not involved in any way with the Hong Kong funds. Stewart had clearly had an independent concern about George's welfare. To him there was nothing wrong with that. George felt that he need not look into it any further.

9. OSCAR

It was how Oscar managed to intimidate his opponents that surprised his teammates. The explanation was partly physical, as he was very tall and broad, plus he worked out in the gym. The rest was down to the nature of verbal exchanges with batters. Some would give as good as they got, others would meekly try to ignore the aggressive comments. He was fast, very fast, in fact recorded in practice at over seventy miles per hour. This was high-speed bowling by any club standard. The ball weighed five and three quarter ounces, creating enough velocity to inflict pain. Oscar would sprint in to bowl and unleash the ball like a wild animal, groaning and snorting. His usual tactic was to deliver the ball full at the feet of the opponent. Some would be quick enough themselves to react, others not so. A ball on the toes would see the person writhe in agony, as it was normally a relatively unprotected area of the body. The very next ball would be fired into the ground so it rose up to the upper body of the batter. It was a classic fast-bowler routine. Any batter unprepared would get hit in the ribcage.

Oscar would then ask of the person, 'Tried to hit it then?', with the opponent doubled up after taking the hit. 'What do you think batter?' Oscar would say again, panting and sweating in front of the batter like some gladiator waiting for a signal.

Ump then would usually intervene. 'All right, bowler, come on, let's get on with it.'

The very next ball would invariably hit the batter's stumps, one of which normally cartwheeled in the air, and the batter was out. It was strange how often this did actually happen.

'That way, mate!' Oscar advised the forlorn opponent, who of course knew the way to the pavilion and did not need reminding. Oscar's friends and family had no idea of the monster in him that was created on the green at the weekend. To them the game was gentle, a quiet and civilised sport, with manners and decorum. They saw it as a good influence. Faro had reported that one batter was so terrified by Oscar that he was visibly shaking with fear whilst standing to receive the ball at the wicket. Not that Faro as the wicket-keeper would be inclined to offer any messages of support to the batter in such circumstances.

After a match Oscar would take his boots off and lie on the grass with his cigarettes and beer, quietly contemplating messages on his mobile phone. Mostly this was trading. Once it used to be anything from commodities, derivatives, even designer watches. Now, however, narcotics offered the best return against the risks involved. He was an intermediary, he neither knew the supplier nor cared. He added a substantial margin and made handsome profits. Oscar saw himself as no worse than City financiers or stockbrokers. As long as there was demand, he would supply his customers. Stewart was his best, at least in the amount of ordering. Now he was an ex-customer and Oscar had worked out the financial consequences of his lost custom very quickly.

Oscar had a day job as a specialist IT consultant. The work he currently had was at Farnborough in relation to defence equipment. It was a government contract and it was reasonably well paid. Computers had always been his thing, at school he cared about nothing else. He was an age when one of the first things he learnt was programming. Essentially, the mathematical theory behind it. First it was a journey of discovery. Then once he had cracked programming, he discovered he had a skill in keeping computer systems secure. He could protect systems from most outside interference from hackers, even overseas belligerent state hackers. However, for his skill level in protecting important defence systems, he felt he was not remunerated enough. Hence his business on the side. Risky, but he covered his tracks very well and remained undetected. Buyers, of course, would never reveal his sales. The suppliers never made direct contact, it was an invisible economy. He would try young people first, teenagers were best. They would seem eager to try and he could draw them in quite successfully over time. He assumed the money must come from parents. It was not hard drugs, recreational stuff only. It was illegal, but that was the attraction as it increased prices. The harder drugs cost more but penalties for being caught increased exponentially. Oscar had applied his own logic to risk and reward and selected his product line accordingly.

Stewart was an unusual customer. It was not just his age that was different but the actual quantities that were strange. But Oscar had no issue with what happened to the stuff, information on which was of no concern to him. Stewart had always been very curious about Oscar's workmates and customers of the business. Funny, as for most people it was a complete bore to them. But Stewart had clearly worked in computers before, at least at some point in his life. He had some good ideas for potential algorithms, which he said he learnt at University. He even wanted to come to the IT fair at Farnborough. It was being held at the same time as the famous air show.

Oscar would drive to his workplace in his second car, which was a dull overseas model. He had another vehicle at home which would, if were to use it, create plenty of notice from the security cordon at Farnborough. The building that constituted work was of a modern design, round and fat-looking, almost like a steel doughnut. After parking, he would walk 50 metres to Level One security, for which he had an electronic tag to gain access. Two corridors of the lifeless modern building would get him to Level Two security, which was permanently manned and which used retina recognition to open the door. He never spoke to the Marine on duty, who would simply stare ahead.

Through to the systems operations centre of the building or the 'jam filling of the doughnut', as his boss liked to call it. The atmosphere here was different – calm and quiet, but with screens showing enough information to run a small airport. He liked that comparison, as his current project was a system to protect the military air traffic systems of the NATO countries. This was something that was not for commercial sale but a highly secret piece of hardware and software to be used by sovereign governments.

The jam filling only had about twenty working there at any one time. Only about thirty people had Level Two access. Whether you had access or not was never discussed with others. *'The ayes have it!'* This was a joke that a workmate had about who could get through the retina check. To enter you had to bring yourself and not a pass or a tag. In fact there was no need for a Marine to be positioned there, so secure was the security procedure. The MOD always wanted to show they were in control and insisted on an armed guard being stationed there. Oscar remembered Stewart would often ask about the presence of military at work. Oscar was not allowed to divulge this but Stewart was a good customer so what the hell. The more co-operative he was the more Stewart seemed to buy from him. This was good business! He was also one of his Saturday teammates, and so he could be trusted not to let on what was going on in the doughnut.

There was an elaborate coffee machine within Level Two. Oscar pressed at the usual buttons and the drink appeared. He added an extra paper cup. It provided better insulation for the walk to his desk. The coffee was placed on a browned stack of notepaper next to his PC, which he turned on.

'Shit!' Oscar shouted out. It was an email from the section chief of the project demanding a meeting. This was bad news. Good news would be communicated in some kind of congratulatory email copied to all in the HR department. Even worse was the time of the meeting which was '*as soon as you open and have read this email*'. Oscar sighed and walked from his desk to request a visit to Level Three. He had no access to Level Three, so this entailed leaving Level Two and then Level One and going on to main security reception to identify himself. Once he had done so and calls were made, he was escorted to Level Three directly, without having to go through Level One and Level Two. That made no logical sense to Oscar, but he wasn't about to bring it up as an issue.

'Ah, Oscar, there you are!'

'You wanted to see me?'

'Yes, come in.' The door was closed behind them.

'Look, we have had a leak. We think it is substantial and we have no choice but to implement wind-down.' He looked stressed. This was serious, and potentially an end to the whole project.

'First, though, we need to establish the source of the hacker.'

'How serious is it?' asked Oscar.

'They have accessed the JAM system — that's how bad it is!'

This was the Jericho Access Matrix computerised communication system, known as JAM for short. Designed as an impenetrable comms system, it was the great hope of NATO central command. Its main objective was to counter Russian interception of signals in the British communications base in Cyprus. This was NATO's gateway to intercepts in the Middle East. Jericho was itself a code name for the nature of the protective walls that were behind the design of the system. Section Chief loved the fact that the title initials were JAM and so the name stuck.

'You are to start now, wind-down to start noon today. I need your initial conclusion today so that I can brief Whitehall.'

'What do we have to go on?' asked Oscar.

'Not a lot, just the password that was entered at the start of the process. It leads to Beijing, but that could be a Russian trick to put us off the scent. The Chinese have been checked out and we don't think it is them. But keep your mind open.'

'Industrial hack?'

'No, I would say not, due to the nature of the entry program. It is very good, specially created.'

The phone rang, the Chief picked it up and Oscar was beckoned away with a wave of the hand.

Wind-down of the JAM system was governed by an emergency protocol known by only a handful of operators. Oscar was one of these. His morning was spent putting this into action. At noon all was done. Now Oscar needed to find the source. It could be seen as closing the stable door after the horse has bolted. However, discovery of the hacker could lead to the discovery of just how compromised the system was and to which potential enemy.

There was not much to go on, other than the Beijing lead, but as the section chief said, it could be a trick. The best assumption was that it was Russian and he would work on that.

By the end of the day he was no nearer the answer but he knew the worst. Substantial amounts of data had been extracted.

The pickings were so rich that it was almost impossible to imagine a penetration on this scale without access to, at the very least, Level One computer systems. He could see why the Chinese theory had been put forward. If any access was made to the central core of the system's program, a screen full of Chinese writing appeared, preventing further access, like a kind of shield. But this was also a program in itself and Oscar later that evening discovered it was transmitting data via the internet.

'What do you mean transmitting?' said the Section Chief to Oscar.

'Exactly that, Chief, it has spread into the system and re-established itself as its own program.'

'How did it get in?'

'Well, sir, that is difficult to answer, but the attack is using a Trojan Horse concept and it had to have been physically brought to this section.'

'What, an inside job?'

'Someone with access to at least Level One, all you need is another laptop or even a large-capacity USB stick.'

'Bloody hell, that means I am going to have Five or Six crawling all over us – or even those weirdo GCHQ fellas.'

'I can contact GCHQ, get ahead of the game?'

'Thanks, but it is out of my hands. I have been roasted by Whitehall and will have to report to some Defence Minister that frankly I have never heard of!'

* * *

As Oscar drove home later that evening, he thought about all of his colleagues, one by one. It was not them, he felt sure. Somehow the section had been entered. But that was another day. He was going home now.

Oscar opened the door into his flat. It was strangely stiff – his kitbag and bat were piled up behind the door. It was then he remembered, some weeks ago on a Sunday, the day after a match, Stewart had phoned to say that he had found his Level One access pass amongst his own kit. It must have fallen out in the pavilion. Oscar felt a cold shiver run down his back. But why would Stewart use his pass? Did he actually use the pass? Oscar turned in for the evening, tomorrow he would run his access detector program to check.

Oscar had devised his computer breach detection program specifically for this type of incident. That is, a breach by direct access rather than remote access. A direct access breach is often seen in movies. The villain (or hero) has just broken into an office and has a few seconds to download data from an opponent's laptop. However, this was in reality an easily detectable intrusion to a system. The real danger to a computer system's integrity was direct access not from a human being but from data entering the system, using what was known in IT as a Trojan Horse virus. Such a device could be capable of collecting and *transmitting* data silently, and not just destroying it.

Oscar arrived at work early and set his program to work. The result came through about an hour later. His own work laptop had been activated and access made through its own USB portal. Bloody hell! It must have been Stewart, and the password would have been easy: WONby3Wickets. It changed every week and on Monday last Oscar changed his password to the result of the weekend match just past. Only Stewart would know that and now he was dead. Hang on a minute, Oscar now checked who else had been accessing the system. In a breach like this a person is doing it either for money or out of a sense of duty. This could be duty to a cause, such as animal rights, or it could be for an overtly political motivation or national cause. In a word, spying. He needed to know how the information was being used and who by. That much he could report to the Chief. The identity of his hacker being his best narcotics customer would have to wait.

Oscar briefed the Chief later that morning in his grand office.

'Chief, I have no doubt in my mind that it is China. It is a TRAWLER device and a very smart one at that. It has all the hallmarks of China intelligence craft.'

This innocent enough phrase – TRAWLER – was in fact an acronym, but it was also descriptive. It stood for a Trojan Raid and Wireless Leaker, an electronic device which itself caused a breach of computer security. By its design it was capable of transmitting out of the computer system it had entered and doing so wirelessly. Sending information to an external host of the contents of the system it had penetrated, it was virtually unde-tectable as an IT security breach. It could and would allow a stream of information to be leaked without the knowledge of the host. It was a technology geek's worst nightmare. China seemingly was leading the world in the art of cyber attacks to gain information of use to it. All western governments directed substantial resources in order to counter this threat.

'Shit, are you sure? I thought we could defend against TRAWLERs?' His boss looked concerned.

'I have never seen one like this, it's still transmitting data,' said Oscar.

'Then it's a call to GCHQ all right. My God, I was due to go on holiday this week.'

'We will also need counter-terrorism at Five to come in on it.'

'Yes, and bloody well Yes. This has got to be closed down, you realise that. And the PM will have to be told. All those JAM systems are compromised now. The Americans will go completely apeshit. Their Pacific Fleet is making a goodwill visit to Hong Kong next month, warship open to the public, exhibition, kids wearing sailor caps – all that crap. The Chinese will be having a great laugh by now.'

'Chief, who will notify them, the US that is?'

'It's out of my hands, this will have to go to the Defence Minister now. I shall make the call, you report back this evening to me. Nobody else, right? Oh and make sure your weekend is free, maybe the one after that as well.'

Oscar had a major breach on his hands and knowledge of who had accessed his computer. This was going to be a rough ride; my God, if he could have got his hands on Stewart right then!

This would take considerable time and skill, but if the TRAWLER was still transmitting he would get to Stewart. This needed to be fast.

10. DANIEL

Though it was clear to Daniel that he liked Angie a lot, he couldn't cope with a child. That was not how it was supposed to turn out. It was a level of commitment too far. And what would the others think? Stewart, he concluded, would have had the worst reaction, as he was very close to Angie. They were like a sexless husband and wife. Daniel was the sex bit for Angie. Was that why it was all so exciting for Angie? The death of Stewart had changed everything. The reaction from Angie was too severe and Daniel couldn't deal with that, cowardly as it may be. He was not the stay-at-home type. Anyhow, all that grieving was too much. How could it affect her that much? It wasn't as if the child had lost a parent. Perhaps it was the fact that she loathed her own father, and Stewart was some type of replacement figure, hence the lack of her sexual interest in him. Daniel could only guess. Anyway, he didn't want kids.

'What the hell do you mean?' said Angie to Daniel later that day. 'Not what you wanted?'

'No,' he replied.

'Well, what the hell do you think we were doing then?'

'Look, I didn't expect any of this, the baby, Stewart dying. I am not ready to be a father.'

'Sod you, what about the life of the child, and me? Don't you give a damn?'

'Yes, absolutely I do, you don't have to go through with this, you know. I will cover costs and that.'

'Cover costs?' Angie looked at him in shock.

'Yes. Just let me know, I . . .'

She answered him before he could finish. 'Just fuck off! Why the hell I was interested in you, God only knows!'

'You didn't seem to mind too much when we made out!'

With that Angie cracked the back of her hand against Daniel's face. She mumbled something inaudible and stood back. It hurt him, he felt ashamed.

There was silence. Daniel wiped his mouth with a cloth from the kitchen.

Angie spoke first, in slow measured tones: 'Now you listen to me. I have learnt these past weeks how . . . how precious life is, and that means I am going to keep and cherish this baby. You clearly value none of that. If you are not prepared to support me with the baby, you go, and go now.'

'Look, I know you are upset about Stewart and all that, it's clearly affecting you in some way.'

'Don't patronise me, don't even try.'

Daniel grunted, turned his back on her and walked to the door.

'Yes, that's right, just walk away from it. You're a bastard!' she screamed at him.

Daniel slammed the door shut. 'I am like your baby then,' he shouted back, and immediately regretted it.

Daniel had never liked Stewart and he liked him even less now, everyone was so cut up about him dying.

Stewart was in the year below him years ago, back at school, and he always seemed a strange kid to him. Daniel was the first to have noticed the darkish tint and slight slant to his eyes. He was also very out of place at the start of the first year, and the teachers made a lot of fuss over him. He didn't go home in the holidays. Always seemed to have had money and the best sports equipment. My, how Daniel made his life hell! It was a real laugh. Stewart was soon known at school as *Grasshopper*. He had grassed up a classmate who had poured ink inside his jacket to a teacher. That was a bad mistake. And he had the misfortune to look like the boy in a martial-arts film popular on TV at the time. The name stuck. Everyone was desperate to be part of a tribe of boys or at least be amongst the teasers. So little Grasshopper was an easy target for those wanting to assert themselves. The verbals would be directed against any friends he had as well. He should have stood up and taken it, but he never did. Daniel never liked him for that either. After a while the teachers turned against Stewart as well. There only on someone else's charity was the rumour. How he ever got to Oxbridge was a mystery. Not deserved, and probably was there by the gift of someone else again. The deputy head of the school had become a tutor at the very college that Stewart applied to.

It was rumoured that it was because of him that he got the place. It must have been horrendous for Stewart at school apart from this one master who showed him a reasonable amount of kindness. but so what? What did that matter? He had had to face the same in the early years.

Daniel's own horror began with his childhood at home, when he was about seven or eight years old. Strange comments were made by his parents first, not seeming to care about him when he got home from preschool at weekends. Then the beatings started. First, it was a bash around the ears when he dropped something. There was a bottle which broke on the kitchen floor and then a spoon of his fell off the dining table. He was hit both times afterwards with no explanation. When he was pushed down the stairs he didn't know anyone was behind him and he hurt his head badly. Then it got worse, much worse. In fact, it was so bad that he didn't want to come home. He had a school friend who said it may be because he was an only child. It didn't make any sense then to Daniel. No sense at all. There was one Sunday morning at home when Daniel felt unwell and did not come down for breakfast. The family always went to church on a Sunday, leaving the house promptly at 10.30am. All had to be up at 9.30am to eat. Daniel was not there at the table, only his mother and father. Daniel, lying on his bed, first heard the sound of feet on the stairs and then he saw the metal poker raised in the air. But what was so different now as compared with the other times was that his mother was smiling as she struck him through the sheets and blankets.

'You are *lazy*, just like your stupid damned father. *Get* up, right *now*.'

There were three heavy blows made with his mother giving extra emphasis on her words 'lazy', 'get' and 'now'. When she had finished, she dropped the smile. Surveying him carefully, she said, 'And don't think your father will help you, stupid shit.'

Daniel's father never did help. The two of them were as keen to send him to boarding school as Daniel was to go. He endured two to three years like this before he was packed off to senior school. Other boys he spoke with there didn't seem to be hit at home by their mother. So he didn't tell anyone any more about it. He never asked friends home in the holidays. They never suggested it either.

Daniel felt better when he could take it out on Stewart. He wasn't going to be the only one, the misery could be shared.

It was almost 25 years later that Daniel and Stewart ended up living in the same town. Daniel had moved out from London where he was an investment banker. He went to a tolerably good university. He possessed flair and had an air of conviction about him which led to various City job offers. The town was close enough to the main line station to be an easy commute to his City desk. Many of Daniel's mates had done a similar thing, although they tended to have got married at the same time. Daniel would move from one girl to another. They would usually say he was difficult to be with. He would say he couldn't really give a damn. If anything, he rather resented them but they were useful to have around, particularly at night. Daniel was tall and extremely good-looking, there was no doubt about that. He also liked to spend. That combination of looks and money so aligned proved to be a successful cocktail, to coin a phrase. Daniel wouldn't normally socialise with Stewart. Not many women knew or hung around him. It was the Club that had brought them together, enjoyment of the game the only thing they had in common. They would keep a distance. Daniel continued to be annoyed about the attention Stewart's death was creating, rather like the attention Angie gave him. He resented this but he knew he could do something about it, by making Angie a conquest! This was different, there was something not right about it and he was going to delve. If Stewart had orchestrated some kind of disappearance, then Daniel would track the man down. He would start at Oxford, at the college shared by Stewart and his old deputy head.

Daniel had been invited to speak at a conference at Oxford Business School. It was too much of an opportunity to miss and so, when the time came, he enquired about his old deputy head at the porter's lodge of his college. It was there he discovered he was now Master of the college. He called in at his lodgings.

'Ah yes my boy, do come in,' said Mr Baraclough, the Master, after a swift introduction by Daniel. On stepping into the lodging's drawing room, he noticed the Master looking at him rather carefully, as if his presence was suspicious.

'My golly, such a long time, a long time. When did you leave Hsarretchester?'

'Just after you had moved up to the position at this college.'

'Well, yes, some years ago indeed. Do come into my study. I had just ordered tea!'

Daniel walked in to the large study area and noticed a foppish young undergraduate sat on an ornate lounge-style chair. He looked uncomfortable with the interruption.

'Do you mind Mr Potter being here?' said the Dean.

It was part question, part statement. Whatever. Daniel simply smiled and reflected on how the old queen had created the perfect life for himself here as Master of an Oxford college. The study was decorated in an assortment of red and some brown tones, lit by lights on the walls fashioned to look like candles. There was a substantial fireplace, above which was a large pen-and-ink sketch of a reclining male nude. The available light from the ornate windows threw a sheen on the sketch. With the light staring to fade, together with the candle-lights, the study had a slightly ethereal aura. Tea was brought in by an under-porter and set out on a large table.

'Awful dammed business about Mr Kilbride,' said the Dean.

Daniel was taken aback by this statement. He had rehearsed on the walk to the college how he would explain that he was making enquiries about Stewart, the circumstances of his death and so on, all of which had now been rather pre-empted.

'Yes, I didn't realise you knew about this.' Daniel again looked up at the picture above the fireplace. There was a flicker of recognition of the man's facial features. It was starting to make a bit more sense now.

'It is very sad, very sad,' continued the Dean, who told Daniel now, in hushed tones, about the fact that it could be revealed that Kilbride (he never used his actual name when talking to Daniel) was working for Her Majesty's Government in Intelligence. Of course, Stewart had made a great personal sacrifice. The Master added that he was originally recruited here in the college. Stewart often discussed it with him at length before accepting the invitation, dangerous as it was. The Master paused as if briefly contemplating those dangers. He went on, 'It was not a tap on the shoulder, like you read in books, of course. People are carefully selected and invited to discuss matters, which he did in my own office back in the days when I was a tutor.'

'If you don't mind me asking, how did you know?'

'About his death?' asked the Dean.

'Yes, that's what I mean. It's just that it's taken a long time for us – people that currently know or rather knew him – to find any information at all about things.'

'Well, I was contacted. I can't tell you why I was but I was visited about the news by the police.'

'I see. So, is there an issue with his death that makes it strange or unusual?'

This seemed to unnerve the Master.

'Now then, sorry, that's confidential. I thought you were probably here to talk about his life, old times, memories and suchlike.'

'Nothing of the sort, old chap! Look, his death is mysterious, it looks like some big conspiracy. Thought you may see a way through it.'

The Master looked nervously about the room.

'I think you should be going now. I have a class I am doing.' He flicked a hand at the seated undergraduate, who for the first time looked smug.

'Well, Master, I think you have confirmed something for me, that is for sure.' With that Daniel left.

On the train journey home Daniel turned his thoughts over. Ideas were racing through his head, flying past like the country-side beside the tracks. He wanted to get Angie back and so Daniel was not going to let this one go. The death of Stewart seemed to have all the characteristics of something underhand. Spies, police involvement and unanswered questions. If Stewart thought he would disappear without trace, then he, Daniel, may have to disappoint him. Whatever is going on he will find it.

That way Angie would come running back. She would discover that she had been deceived by that perfect gentleman, Stewart. All that pain she had endured so far. She would then come back to him as before.

II. STEWART

His mother was Alice Kathryn Stewart, who was born at number 7 Sandiefield Road in the Gorbals area of Glasgow. One of Alice's earliest childhood memories was the day the man from the Landlord came to make them leave their house. It was cold and they had to stand in the street. Gran lived with them and she was too ill to remain upright. The Landlord's man said they all had to go because the house was coming tumbling down. For many years after that she would remember vividly her Gran's howls of pain from having to walk a long way in the cold. Alice had asked her Mum, 'Where are we going?' They would go to the Kirk, they would be safe there, replied her mother. The Kirk was a large Victorian brick building. It was near the railway station and so its outside walls were dirty. The bricks were red in colour, if you looked close. It was warm inside and other families were there, things were shared. Nothing was their own, as it was before in their house.

Childhood after that saw movement from place to place, different parts of the City. The areas she used to play in with friends, often derelict open spaces, had new homes and blocks built. They never had a new home. They lived in old places, cramped and dark. That was what she remembered anyway.

Years later, when she was 15 years of age, Alice got work as a cleaner for a Scots member of the Kirk. Her own mother told her not to work for English people. It was their fault that we all lived like we did. The Landlord was English, he didn't live in Glasgow but in London. Alice shivered instinctively when she thought back to that freezing day when they were forced to leave their own house.

Alice soon earned enough to both help her mother and to buy her own food. This was better than to be handed it at the Kirk. Cleaning was hard but good work. Soon she moved on and was retained with a good reference by another respectable Scottish family. She had a room of her own in the house and one day off every three weeks. Alice's Mum said she was so proud and that they were a fine family to be in the service of. The came the day when Alice's mother died. Her mother's last words to her on the day she died was to tell her daughter to always stand up for herself and follow her heart. Alice never forgot those words.

Hard work led to more advancement. Soon she had one of the rooms which had electric light. Alice was able to read and did so late every night. She loved books from the very first time Gran used to read to her before bedtime.

The house was on Great Western Road, Glasgow, a place she had always contemplated as if it was some rich far distant land. But she was here now living there. The family she worked for had five children whom she adored, four girls and one baby boy. They used to say her work pinafore made her look like Alice in Wonderland, just like the pictures in the book. Soon it was clear that Alice was more housekeeper than house cleaner. The change was gradual, but pivotal was her relationship with the children.

One morning she was called to see the master of the house, Mr Kilbride. Something was wrong or at least out of the ordinary.

'You wanted to see me, sir?'

'Alice, look, we are having to move. In fact, we are going to Hong Kong to live. I have been appointed to a position out there, a permanent position with the Bank.'

'Oh, I see. All of you, and the children?' She didn't know where it was but she could sense from his demeanour that it was a long way away.

'Yes, all the family. But, look, I have been asked to tell you . . .' He paused.

'Yes, sir?'

'To ask you, Alice, if that's all right . . .' He looked very worried suddenly. 'Look, we want you to come with us. Well, you know, the children want you to come and it wouldn't be the same without you! You will come, will you?'

Alice was shocked at first and asked for time to decide. She wept when she got to her room. She prayed and wanted to speak to her Mum. For God's sake, my girl, what are you waiting for? was the answer. When you are there, follow your heart, my sweet lassie.

* * *

Three months later Alice started the journey with the Kilbrides from the Glasgow docks. That journey and the arrival in Hong Kong were exciting and thrilling days. She often told Stewart about that arrival.

Sailing into the entrance to Hong Kong harbour not long after dawn was like looking at a scene from an exotic Hollywood movie. Boats of all kinds were everywhere, from large barges to small sailing rigs. Horns and hooters were blaring as the Star Ferry ships carved their way through the mass of assembled craft. Traders in what looked like canoes were selling wares to passing boats. This included such varied items as wooden carvings and live chickens squawking in a cage. Alice had never seen anything like it.

The process of disembarking took some time. It was only then that Alice felt the heat for the first time. It was like entering a boiler room, intense and soporific. Her clothes were wrong but she had nothing else, well, not yet anyway. The Kilbride family then had to travel further. The residence for the family was to be high up in the Peak above Victoria, on Hong Kong Island. The journey to the house involved steering the children through crowds of people, all seemingly shouting orders, all of which were unintelligible to Alice. Then on to another boat. The children dutifully followed Alice as the luggage was attended to by numerous porters, each arguing about who was first to take on the task. As the entourage went up to the Peak, the air became cooler. It was like opening a window and gasping fresh air.

Most of Alice's time was spent high up on Hong Kong Island, at first she rarely ventured out of the house grounds. It was her lust for reading and learning that led her to the Kowloon Institute book club. This was held on a Tuesday evening, and coincided with her free evening, which was now once a week. On those evenings she would walk to the Peak funicular at around 5 o'clock, then picking up a Star ferry at the bottom of the hill to Kowloon side. It was then only a walk of a couple of blocks to the Institute from the ferry terminal. There was where all that the life in the Peak was not. It was hot and loud and generally untidy. A mass of humanity all going about their daily lives. General traders, grocers and meat suppliers competed for space with entertainers and call girls. Alice found these trips invigorating. It was one of the few things that she did for herself. The weekly class was convened by a retired university professor and was diverse in its student make-up. Alice met Molly on her first evening. Molly worked for a household also on the Peak. As well as domestics, there were students, bank clerks, shop-keepers, and numerous civil servant, and they all came from differing ethnic backgrounds. It was Molly who first introduced Alice to Bernie Lee.

Alice had noticed him at an early meeting. Bernie was Hong Kong Chinese and he possessed dark and thoughtful eyes. At least this was what she told Molly. The attraction was physical as well as intellectual. He was a student in politics at the University and Alice would talk with him at a level she rarely achieved in the confines of the Peak. Bernie was not his real name but that which his Cantonese name roughly translated to in terms of sound. The attraction was mutual and much of her free time would be spent with him. Bernie was kind and attentive. Although she had no complaints about her treatment at the Kilbrides, any attention given to her was issued sparingly, even perhaps only by way of a sense of duty. With Bernie it was unconditional.

'You tell me nothing about where you come from,' he would say.

Alice would laugh, 'My life is here in Hong Kong. My past doesn't matter.'

'We are all set by where we came from and what we search for.'

'Well, you tell me where you come from then!' More laughter.

'I am Chinese and that is my beacon. I believe in the Chinese society and my goal is to achieve it one day here in this place.' The danger of these statements made him even more alluring.

'So you want the British to go from here?'

'Go they shall, it is just a question of time. The mainland lease will come to an end. Look at the tensions in Macau, the Portuguese can't wait to move out!'

As a student at the University, he was active in the politics of the institution itself. He also stood for liberty and workers' rights in the face of what he regarded as imperialist suppression. To Alice, he was different from anyone else she had met. His political leanings had resonance with her humble childhood and memories of hard-bitten absentee landlords.

Alice's mother had told her to follow her heart. That had led to Bernie and after some months she knew that it was going to be permanent.

The day that Alice told her employer that she was engaged to be married was as difficult as it was awkward. She had realised that this revelation meant that her work at the Kilbride's would come to an end, but it was the hostility to her choice of husband for which she was unprepared. The light-hearted 'Who is the lucky fella then?' delivered with a smiling face, turned to darker concern when she explained he was a Chinese student living in Kowloon. That the person she loved was a native (in their eyes) was a shock to them, as was their reaction to Alice. She was even told that the children were not to know. They gave her a month's wages and bade her farewell. Despite many requests, Alice was not provided with a reference. Tragically, some months later the Kilbride boy contracted typhus fever and died, bringing more anguish to the family, for he was their only son.

Even if it was the early sixties, for a woman without qualifications or references the opportunities for work in Hong Kong colonial society were scarce. So her life became that of Bernie and his political journey. For that is what it was, the destination ultimately being a unified China. They lived in a small apartment in Kowloon with little money but with big ambitions.

Alice and Bernie's son was born, and Alice chose his first name after the name of her own family, the Stewarts. This was important to her and Bernie understood. So her past was able to be present here in the form of her own dear Stewart Lee.

Bernie, soon after his graduation, secured a senior teaching post at a Chinese-speaking school and after two years was deputy head and then later headmaster of Chung Wah Middle School. Alice was finally truly content and cherished those five years of happy but modest family life. Then came the 1967 Hong Kong riots, and her life was to change once more.

There had been a foretaste of problems in 1966, when there were increased tensions in Hong Kong industrial relations. The rates of pay and length of hours worked had seen little change for decades. The tension that had been brewing in Hong Kong during the 1950s increased in the 1960s, with frequent strikes and even violent disorder. As pay was low, the cost of Hong Kong products was substantially undercutting the equivalents from the US and Europe, where pay was gradually rising. Hong Kong had become, since the end of World War Two, the major factory for the world supply of light industrial items, toys, gifts and smaller engineered products. Unbelievably, the majority of workers were still paid piecemeal. This was particularly the case with nearly all women workers and there was also no legal upper limit on working hours. This had helped to fuel the success of Hong Kong as a place of efficient low-cost manufacture, but it was at a human cost, and a perfect storm was about to break. The adverse conditions combined together. First was the role of China itself and the Cultural Revolution with its hopelessly misnamed 'Great Leap Forward', leading to huge waves of migrants crossing the border to Hong Kong. The Colony struggled to cope with basic infrastructure needs: housing, education and, of course, medical.

Living conditions were horrendous for migrants. These people were desperate and so would accept willingly the concept of pay by amount of production. Employers took advantage of an over-supply of compliant labour. The Colony population continued to rise dramatically. Then the storm broke.

The key players in the crisis which erupted in the months of April through to September 1967 were workers with no reason-able alternative to going on strike, their trades unions, employers of course and also (sensing disorder and anarchy) the state in the form of the Hong Kong Police (HKP). During April 1967 a strike in a factory that manufactured artificial flowers, the San Po Kong Artificial Flower Factory, was to be the start of months of unrest and strikes. Bernie became involved in the Anti-British Communist Struggle Group (AB Group), the aims of which were to return Hong Kong to China and to effect lasting change in workers' rights. It was a bitter irony that China itself had helped to create the conditions that led to such alleged menace. The Flower Factory strike was significant as it had attracted attention of the Beijing leadership, following particularly violent disorder on 6 May 1967. Then on 15 May 1967 a written diplomatic protest was delivered to British diplomats at the chargé d'affaires in Beijing, concerning the violence that had occurred outside the Flower Factory. It demanded release of detainees and payment of compensation. China believed that the violence was unprovoked and instigated against workers. The HK Government had inter-vened at the Flower Factory by ordering the HKP to embark on a policy of arresting and detaining strikers at will.

Bernie himself decided enough was enough and by this point was in the leadership of the AB Group. This was the moment, he believed, for the workers of Hong Kong to unite together. He had seen a precedent set about a year before in the Portuguese colony of Macau. After great tension and intervention from China, Portugal did indeed leave Macau in 1966 to the authority of China, the pressure being both diplomatic and otherwise.

The AB Group would organise protests against British direct rule with the backing of trades unions. This was mostly in the form of demonstrations and the release of propaganda. There was a general strike that began on the 23 June 1967, which involved no less than twenty separate unions and lasted four days. Then in July and August there were more violent protests and the protestors' tactics changed to that of a bombing campaign. For Bernie, it was a change for the worse, as he sensed it would unleash the Imperial force against them. Explosives and bomb threats would not achieve the change he desired. An organised but rather restrained approach by the Hong Kong Governor to law and order had been witnessed so far. Bomb attacks needed different tactics. Bomb threats were first limited to Government installations and police stations. Then came the death of innocents on 21 August 1967 by a bomb explosion in a crowded civilian area. Hong Kong was tense, with the Governor's office sensing danger in China's ambiguous stance on the legitimacy of its rule. The Governor's office reacted by declaring a state of emergency, and the British army were mobilised to work alongside the HKP.

Bernie had nothing to do with bombings but he was actively raising funds for striking workers and would organise attention to their social and even medical needs, but his name appeared on a wanted list. Wanted because the Colonial power was frightened of what he was capable of achieving. He was picked up during the dramatic military/police joint operation in the North Point district of Hong Kong Island. Jutting into Kowloon Bay, the district was close to moored Royal Naval ships with military support.

The incident was reported in the local press the next day, particularly well covered in HK Government sanctioned papers under dramatic headlines:

AIRBORNE SMASH AND GRAB
NETS STRIKE ACTIVISTS

Acting on intelligence, specially trained teams of the Hong Kong Police with naval helicopters in support made a surprise landing on the roof of the Qiaoguan building at North Point in which militant strike protest organisers were holding an unlawful meeting. Members of the banned group Anti-British Strike Group known as The Twelve were arrested at great personal risk on the part of the well trained police. The detainees were then transferred by helicopter to HMS Hermes anchored in Kowloon Bay with its support fleet. No further information is known on the identity of the detainees. A police spokesperson revealed that a catastrophic violent event was being planned when the police intervened and Hong Kong was now safe from the threat.

Quantan Daily 23 August 1967

The paper failed to report to the public at any time on the fate of the detainees. There was no editorial discussion on the loss of liberty on the part of The Twelve. If an investigation was made at that time, readers could have been made aware that it was to be the Mount Street Detention Centre for The Twelve, and then the notorious Morrison Hill prison building.

Was it a crisis? In reality there was real and present information from MI6 sources that China was ready to invade Hong Kong at any moment. It was clear that, roused by success in Macau, China would use the excuse of the suppression of workers as the reason for action, regardless of world opinion. China at that point was perhaps at its most isolated in terms of global influence. But they held back and the Colony breathed again. The Twelve were then forgotten.

All of The Twelve detainees were interrogated over the course of many weeks. When Bernie was first allowed visitors during September 1967, the riots crisis was passing. The Emergency Regulations allowed detention without trial and, with the absence of key figureheads, industrial relations gradually eased. Ironically, the UK Government of the time considered the HKP as pivotal in saving the Colony from doom. It was from then that they were to be known as the *Royal Hong Kong Police*.

On the first allowed visit in detention Alice took Stewart, then only five years old. Stewart was troubled by the experience and was confused. Alice felt Bernie had aged considerably. She couldn't take Stewart anymore and he was never to see his father again. Bernie Lee was many years later to die in a Hong Kong gaol. The official report stated that a fight had broken out and he with others launched an escape attempt. There was no body delivered up, and no explanation as to what happened to it. Alice's misery was compounded by stonewalling by the HKP and then by the Governor's office. Her life would now be devoted to Stewart, her special boy. Alice vowed that she would ensure that he continued his father's journey. During Bernie's imprisonment Alice received money from the AB Group. There was enough for her and Stewart to live on without her having to leave him whilst working. That was, if she could get a job. Alice was too desperate to question the origin of the money. They looked after her as if she was one of their own.

Some years later Alice was pleasantly surprised when the Kilbride family made contact out of the blue. They had heard of Alice's circumstances and made a generous offer to support Stewart's education. Mr Kilbride had lost his only son at a young age and still had the poor fellow's name down at Hsarretchester School. Kilbride had confided that to be able to send Stewart to Hsarretchester would ease his pain. This was a decision Alice thought long about, as Kilbride had one condition attached to his offer. Stewart would have to take the Kilbride surname as his own. Realistically, Alice was never going to refuse the offer even with this stipulation. How could she turn such an offer down? It would be the best for her son even if it meant Stewart losing her husband's own name. She was also losing her beloved Stewart to boarding at a famous public school in England. She consoled herself that he must learn from the inside if he was to defeat them. This much his father had said to her from his prison cell.

After attending Hsarretchester, Stewart continued his education about the unnerving tradition of the English privileged classes at Oxford University, where he first read PPE and later Oriental Languages. He was able to meet with the future cream of society in the common rooms and in gatherings of college clubs. They all listened heartily to his colonial tales. From there he was introduced by his Philosophy tutor to the Secret Intelligence Service (MI6) at almost exactly the time, in the 1980s, that the British Prime Minister had agreed a treaty for the return of Hong Kong sovereignty to China by the year 1997. Opportunities were seen by MI6 for the gathering of intelligence, particularly on China's intentions going forward. It was deeply ironic that Stewart's first Service posting was to be as an assistant in the Hong Kong desk, working together with the Royal Hong Kong Police. Stewart Kilbride was now firmly within the establishment in Hong Kong.

PART II: THE RECKONING

I

The oak tree on the Graysmere green had seen most things over its 250-year history. It stood tall opposite the pavilion, its branches and leaves acting almost like a protective cloak. It had also seen its share of traitors, one of whom was hanged from its own branches in 1815. This was on a decision of a local assizes court amidst political turmoil in Europe. The pavilion now was being prepared for an end-of-season evening event – the Stewart memorial dinner. If only we could ask the old tree's opinion of that!

June had volunteered to clean and set up the pavilion in readiness. Alan was the first to arrive to open up the bar, turn power on, flick switches, turn various taps.

'Hullo, June. Takes me back to two months ago, when you first told me about Stewart.'

'Making things nice like then. Haven't seen you at church recently – been away?'

Alan paused before answering. 'Not really, I'm just taking stock of things, if you like.' He changed the subject. 'How are we doing for seating?'

'Well, if you ask me, we need more than just them chairs over there!' She pointed at a collection of stacked chairs. Alan nodded. The pavilion annexe had more of the same. Many would come this evening, Alan concluded, and so went in search of chairs. He walked out of the room just as Farokh came in carrying foil-wrapped metal trays of various Asian delicacies. He was putting down and arranging the trays on the long table when Alan returned. Alan acknowledged his friend with a wave of the hand.

'Hi, Alan, I have his favourites here!' he said.

'And mine as well, Faro, excellent stuff.'

'I have more.' Faro turned and went back to his car.

More of the team then arrived at the pavilion and headed into the bar area. It was getting dark now end of summer light was fading.

A slow rumble was heard outside and storm clouds were just visible gathering in the heavens. Light rain fell, and then heavier, dancing loudly on some further foil-covered trays. Faro ran in with them to avoid getting wet himself.

'That's the last of them. Good that the season is over – this is serious rain!' he said to nobody in particular.

The rest of the team arrived sporadically in the next half hour. Angie, one of the last to arrive, had noticeably put on weight. Of course, none of the assembled males had noticed or indeed worked out why. It was left to June, who had decided to stay for a drink at the behest of Alan.

'Oh, my dear!' she exclaimed. 'My, you are looking well. Blooming, if I may say. Can I get you a chair? You must be tired, love.'

This brought out a remarkable attention makeover of at least three of the team who all rushed to the replenished stack of chairs.

'There is really no need for fuss of any kind, but thanks anyway.' With that Angie sat up at the bar.

The noise of voices in the room was getting louder but the sound of the thunder could still be heard.

Kerr crackk, crack-boom!

Alice had left Mount Street Detention Centre just before dark and had to walk to the nearest bus stop. It was two months after Bernie's arrest and it was typhoon season, the start of the heavy rains. Rain started to fall hard on her head and face as she walked. The Centre had been hot. The sensation outside on her body was invigorating for a short time. Soon her wet clothes started to stick uncomfortably to her skin, and she was now getting cold. The journey was longer as she had to divert to go and collect her toddler son, Stewart. She walked with her eyes closed as the rain fell harder and blew into her face. Then she noticed a figure standing beside her. He said something such as step into this, or something similar. It was a kind voice, she did remember that. The umbrella was gigantic, it easily covered them both. The bus shelter was now probably only about five hundred yards ahead but she couldn't see anything in the downpour. As she looked down at the pavement, the rain water poured along its edges. The drains couldn't cope and her feet were now getting very wet. When the shelter at last provided cover she turned to thank the person, but she was alone. The rain was stopping.

The effect of the thunder on the gathering was akin to a starting pistol for a race. The noise outside and the heavy rain led to amused conversations. The party had started.

'Oh, my Lord, we may be stuck here all night!' said Leon.

'I'm happy with that! The bar is well stocked and we have food,' laughed Edmund.

A general tide of relief and goodwill spread around the room. The fun had indeed started. All those expected were there in good time. All the team, that is, except Daniel, who was absent. There were hugs and howls of amused recognition as further people arrived from the Club, including members of the fourth team. Any excuse for a drink. They were known less for their sporting achievements than for those in bars around the county. Soon numerous beer-filled jugs were placed on a trestle table, the type often found at primary schools, except with differing contents. A glass of rosé wine was being slowly consumed by Angie sitting up at the bar, with a glass of water beside it.

Alan said a few words to the gathered team (albeit there was one of their number missing) and to the assembled other members of the Club. There was a toast. All agreed that Stewart would like to have been here – it was his sort of evening! Tomas suggested a trophy be played for in Stewart's honour. Leon thought the trophy a good idea but to be given for best young player of the season. Others from the Club then continued to arrive piecemeal and the atmosphere began to get noisy. A few smokers walked outside. Music was now playing. It was very jolly, as Stewart could himself see from his spot outside, where he had now stood without any movement for some time.

Inside the food was about to be consumed.

'Yes, Stewart would certainly have liked this!' said Edmund, but Oscar couldn't quite hear the comment.

'He would have approved of this feast!' said Oscar.

'Sure, that's what I said, mate!'

Alan had another drink, as George was now walking around serving beer from the jugs. The party then generally hovered over the food trays, paper plates in hand. At about 9 o'clock Daniel arrived, much to the surprise of Alan, who in any event was pleased to see him.

Stewart moved further away from the shadow of the oak tree. Tomas whilst smoking outside had looked in his direction but didn't seemed to have noticed him there. Stewart remembered from training years ago that lighting and taking a cigarette would have the effect of temporarily but considerably reducing a person's night vision. He was in no hurry, in any event. He knew that the action that he was about to take would expose him for ever. This would end most of his adult life wrapped in espionage. All done for the sake of satisfying Beijing's thirst for knowledge about the operations and life of the west. Dutifully and without question to the memory of his father. This was soon to end.

IV

It was the nature of public-school education which for Stewart was the most revealing about the British upper classes. First of his observations was how he had witnessed the collective and stubborn refusal to accept anyone in their midst who was a threat to equilibrium. As an outsider who looked vaguely Eastern, Stewart was initially ostracised at school. However, the adoption of the mantle of the Kilbride name was like a cloth of gold. Slowly, the association of the name with material wealth changed perceptions of him. Stewart might be of use to them, so he would be tolerated. How he resented this. But like a prisoner who had the Hobson's choice of either starving (emotionally at least) or receiving food (metaphorically, through social acknowledgment), he decided to take the comfort of it willingly. The names of the families of the worst perpetrators of this charade were carefully logged in his mind for future use.

Second observation was the preposterous illusion that somehow pupils were privileged merely by their arrival at the school. How being a Hsarrat – as it was known internally – conferred on the fortunate boy a particular notch or significant step up in society without any attempt on that person's part to deserve such an accolade.

Third, and finally, the fact that money could buy such advancement and therefore the pursuit of wealth would for that person be the path to successful progression in life. This last piece of the jigsaw would be reinforced not only in school time but also at home during school holidays. For Stewart, a visit to his mother in Hong Kong during holidays was very rare indeed. There was one Christmas and then a summer visit over all the years he was at school. Instead he went to Scotland to the Kilbride family estate. What could be more normal or easier? The life and times of Lee started to fade away and the Kilbride persona became all-embracing. Who was deceiving who? After all, he had been invited to this particular party and with it came this education. The groundwork was set for him to work for the cause of Communism. Stewart was conscious that this was a path that other of his countrymen had pursued. Each of those had had some success, but many also became disillusioned. Why should that discourage him? This was a different age. His first operational handler in China had asked him this very question, as if treachery had gone out of fashion or was of no use to anyone. Stewart saw himself as very useful if it could lead to the destruction of old problems. Of these he would start with class divide, then privilege and also lack of social morality. Stewart would do his duty for the PRC. Both his mother and father would expect no less of him. But he had some old scores to settle as well along the way. For spitefulness and inhumanity would not go unpunished. Stewart saw himself as someone who would let actions be his guide. Time elapsed made no difference to him and those people would have to face the consequences of their own misdeeds. Hidden as he would be, behind the shadows and able to glide unnoticed.

V

The local town police station not far from the green was functional enough. Built in the 1970, it resembled some kind of nuclear fallout shelter. At least as one would have imagined such a place. The station itself was not manned full time. If any incident occurred after 11pm, then it would be transferred to the next county. It had been open when the informant visited to discuss the matter of Stewart. He was following up a phone call made previously. At the station they were given the information about a likely location for a re-appearance. It was to be the Club pavilion. Unfortunately for them, the station staff treated the matter as if it was a missing person being found. This involved particular forms which should have been filed on any original disappearance. The station had no such form or details of the person. The informant who had visited the local station tried to impress the urgency of the situation. The station duty sergeant emailed regional HQ that a person had reported a likely appearance from the dead of a person who also, for good measure, was a foreign spy. This provoked a telephone call back from regional headquarters. Somewhat abruptly, the local station was soon ordered to expect a visit from the Military Police barracks in Chichester within the hour. The station sergeant thought it strange that such a fuss was being made about very little. His station could make the area secure for the purposes of any local security incident. But he was told that there were regulations specially established for this type of threat and was now under the control of a Gold commander from the Met. The suspect potentially had government secrets and was likely to be dangerous. Under no circumstances was the suspect – also known as the target – to be apprehended before he entered the likely destination. A positive identification could first be made by the informant, the sergeant was told.

Soon Military Police officers arrived in the town, together with a Metropolitan police firearms squad with substantial back-up. Positions were taken by them all around Graysmere, well in advance of the evening. Stewart was able to observe this from a distance with a pair of field binoculars. It made no difference to him, the die was cast. But the identity of the person respon-sible for leaking information about his appearance did intrigue him. Stewart was certain that nobody had recognised his intended actions or indeed had recognised him. Clearly, he had either given an indication of some type or had been monitored at all times. Still, the fact he would be here this evening could be nothing more than an educated guess. Stewart had avoided elec-tronic devices for sometime and had a sophisticated routine for avoiding being followed without him being aware. Which meant it was someone in the team who had revealed his intentions. So

Stewart was lying in wait just as much as they were for him. Would the person be present tonight and how would they betray him? In front of everyone or silently without giving any sign?

He looked at his watch, it was nearly time for this moment to arrive.

VI

Alice wouldn't say she found religion, but rather that it found her. At her lowest point in Hong Kong the Mission was there to save her. First, it was one of various places that agreed to take Stewart and offer childcare whilst she visited the Mount Street Detention Centre. After time she would talk to the nuns before leaving. She usually had little time for chat of any kind but they would listen without judgment. They would also not come out with constant questions. She was still interrogated at every visit she made to Mount Street. That was not the official version of events but the questioning amounted to the same thing in the end. The priest in residence at the Church of Our Lady was Irish. A good man, who was principled, fair but firm. Alice admired the Church and its work in times of crisis, something her mother had taught her. After some months through teaching with the priest she came to understand Mary the mother of Christ not as some mild, angelic character but instead as a mother who was strong and robust in the face of adversity. This meant so much to Alice. On her being received into the Catholic Church in 1968, she was given a rosary and a crucifix. Years later this very cross, after finding a suitable necklace chain, she gave to Stewart when he turned 18. He was about to go up to Oxford.

'Take this with you, it shall protect you.'

'It is beautiful but not something I believe in, you know that.' He looked into his mother's eyes.

'Stewart, my boy, it is a gift from me to you, it is very important to me.' She clasped his hand. When he left for Oxford he replied to his mother that this was a perfectly good reason for him to keep it.

When he returned for Christmas his enthusiasm had diminished. The following year, visiting again at Christmas, he said to Alice that it was time for the crucifix to be returned.

'It is important for this to come back to you now. It will not protect me and I would like you to have it.'

Alice was visibly shocked. 'Why is that, may I ask you?'

'You know my views on religion and it is something I don't uphold. We should believe in the people as one whole, devote all attention to the best service to the people.'

'You sound like your father, it has done him no good. That weird tattoo he made you have – what's that all about?'

'What he wanted to achieve will be achieved, I know that.'

'That's fine for you to say that but what about me? You swan off to Oxford and I am left here. We rely on others' charity. Handouts. What sort of life is that?'

'It's not about you, me or the two of us. There is a wider struggle that we have to deal with.'

'Well, words are all very well, but it does nothing for me.

The only solace I get is from my faith, and that it was there for me.' Alice cried and composed herself. ' I shall always love you but my faith is now my life and clearly not yours. So things will never be the same.'

With that Stewart had left. Only later, when they became the last words that Alice ever said to her son, did he sense the grief that his mother must have then had. His tutor at Oxford told him solemnly about his mother's death. It was a shock but was delivered to him compassionately. And with that he was parentless, his only connection in the mortal world being a small box of assorted belongings. His secret life was about to begin. Maintaining the name Kilbride as a last name caused less difficulty and it was how he was known in England. The Lee in him must be put to one side.

The posting in Hong Kong came with access to various clubs, invites to dinners and the like. His recruitment by the other side in Hong Kong went along the usual lines. Eighteen months of observation of the newcomer passed by, then Beijing marked him out as a loner and someone who could or should be picked off carefully like a delicate fruit from a tree. It was time for them to commence the turn. He was followed one Friday morning to his usual coffee bar on the way to Government House for a routine meeting. It was a fresh spring day, busy with commuters.

A smartly dressed female sat opposite him and with consummate charm began a conversation. It really was quite flattering to him, she was rather beautiful. Stewart considered afterwards that they must have rated him highly. It amused him. He would not fall for that. As there was not the remotest sexual interest on his part, the meetings evolved into a pleasant intellectual dual. It was funny to observe her tradecraft in adapting to the situation. My, how he could have played her for the sake of HM Government and secured an early promotion!

Their dinner at the Colonial Club Hotel was the turning point. For him to raise the stakes by suggesting to her (Anna was her name) an hotel meet-up created a sense of theatre that excited him. Stewart arrived early and walked the lobby inspecting its layout. There was the reception desk, flowers arranged alongside it, lifts by the gift shop. He then saw a large leather upright chair positioned next to a table at one end of the lobby. This was perfect, from it he could see all entrances. Also it was suitably close to the bar for him not to stand out. What Stewart did not know for sure (but suspected) was that his dinner date was in fact one of the most experienced and best operative agents that China had for turning British government officers. Known by the British under the code name of Janus, Anna had been absent from Hong Kong for some time. Schooled in Hong Kong and then enrolled at its University, she gained a first in Economics. Then she sat a master's degree in Politics at the London School of Economics, where MI5 had first noticed her. She gained another first. Now she had re-appeared in the Colony, a fact that Stewart had not reported to his MI6 section chief. He had to be sure it was her. There was fun to be had in discovering this.

Stewart saw the first, and then the second minder arrive into the hotel lobby. This added weight to her credentials. Her own arrival was soon afterwards. It was a confident and self-composed movement as she crossed the lobby towards him. Jet-black hair hung loosely around her shoulders on to a red dress. Heels gently tapped at the marble floor. Enough sound to create her own kind of music as she continued to walk across to him. Then a kiss on the cheek with the aroma of heavy perfume lingering in the air.

'Shall I order the usual?' Stewart asked.

'Why not, it's never too early!' she replied with a smile and sat in the chair opposite him.

The conversation was always very easy between them. She had established he was single and unattached relatively early on. A major barrier was thus out of the way for her. Then would follow her particular tradecraft. Interestingly, although they would be executed very differently, Stewart was trained to use such methods himself. First, the objective would be to root out anxieties or uncertainties at the target's place of work. Then, the general situation in the person's personal life outside that of the office. In particular, such matters as settling in the Colony, housing challenges and so on. Finally, to use the information that had been gleaned as a lever. Stewart playfully defended his own position according to his training. A verbal sparring match around the intricacies of Government House and his apartment downtown.

Having finished their drinks, they stood up and with laughter moved on to eat. It could continue there.

The dinner was at a central table in the hotel's main restaurant. An elegantly presented table with white tablecloth, four wine glasses, cutlery and condiments. The maître d'hôtel held back the chair for Anna and they both sat down. For Stewart this was the perfect moment. There was a romantic intensity about the scene and the evening. So at some point after the first course, when the pianist began gently to play at a baby grand, the direction of the evening's conversation changed. During a fairly innocent discussion on wine to the tune of *Autumn Leaves*, Stewart suddenly began to speak to Anna in Punti, which was a local Cantonese dialect. He had done his checks on Anna's background and knew she would understand the dialect. A form of communication that he also knew well. A glance around beforehand at other diners reassured Stewart that the conversation would remain totally discreet. The wine waiter possibly could make out what was said, but he was not in the room at that point. Stewart began. There was no obvious reaction from Anna at first. Then she suddenly dropped her smile and was studying Stewart intently. She moved closer to his face now with her elbows rested on the table. The silence ended with Anna then sitting back and smiling again, recommencing the conversation, in the same dialect and which Stewart answered as follows:

Anna: You surprise me, you really do mean what you have just said.

Stewart: I don't know why it should be a surprise to you when my father was one of The May Storm Twelve.

Anna: A fact that I have only recently become aware of
  – you have hidden your past well. I have to know that
  you are genuine.

Stewart: That is for you to decide, but I can tell you that
  my past is also my present. I intend it to be my future
  as well.

Anna: So I suppose the question is whether you are prepared
  to assist the People's Republic?

Stewart: That is why you are here with me, is it not?

Anna (whispering): I must know all about you if I am to
  pass you on to your handler.

Stewart: Then ask me what you need to know.

After that the conversation switched back to English for the
rest of the evening. Later, the dinner concluded, they both moved
on via the hotel bar. Anna suggested her apartment for the rest
of the night and Stewart politely declined. He did though accompany her home in the taxi, telling her that it was to ensure her
safety. They both wished each other good night and with that
the recruitment was secured of an active double agent for the
People's Republic of China. In fact, Chinese intelligence training
officers of the future would tell new recruits about the tactics in
the turning of this agent. It was quoted in PRC training manuals
that the success of the play to secure the services of Kilbride
was '[a] unique one-off event unlikely to be repeated in such a
manner again'. Stewart was rather pleased with that assessment.

VII

Stewart was now thinking back to that time. It meant so much to him then. Strangely, Anna had meant a lot to him despite the deception that both were engaged in. But the future which he then saw had proved to be very different once it had unravelled itself.

Rain continued to pour heavily down on the green. There was a crack of thunder. He instinctively moved closer up, near to the trunk of the old tree. Should he stay under the tree? It wasn't safe in case lightning struck this area. He then contemplated what it was that he was now giving up — was it simply the cause of Communism, or was it his old life? Stewart felt into his jacket pocket and held the object there in his hand. He had never worn the crucifix since his mother died. He wanted it with him now and wanted to handle it. This seemed comforting. He placed it back in his pocket.

Oscar had now moved inside. Further music, considerably louder now, could be heard from the pavilion. Stewart contemplated how all would recognise him as he was now. The disguise had gone, he was ready — this was the moment.

Stewart walked across the wet grass, head bowed into the collar of his trenchcoat, and on to the pavilion steps. Without pausing, he walked in through the door.

The effect of the appearance of Stewart Kilbride to those who thought he was lost for ever was not instant. Loud voices in mid-flow slowly calmed, conversations ended gradually. It was like a fairground attraction closing down for the day and taking time to splutter to a halt. As if small leaves were slowly falling off a tree until finally bare — it seemed like time had stopped for that long. The music had momentarily stopped to give the whole entrance a sense of drama. Another song was ready on the turntable but someone then turned the music off. A sea of faces were taking in what they could see. No one could remember afterwards who actually saw Stewart first or who spoke the first words to him.

Tomas had moved forward instinctively. 'Shit, what the . . . ?' he said.

'Stewart, is that you?' Alan asked as if Stewart was obscured far away in the distance.

Angie moved slowly forward, easing herself off the bar stool. She looked pale as if she had seen a ghost. Apart from these three, nobody else had moved. They all stared in unison at the figure by the door.

'I guess you probably want a drink!' said George, which seemed to break the tension.

Then Angie intervened: 'You bastard, you sodding bastard! How could you do this to me, Stewart?' Angie was shouting now as she continued to move forward. Once in front of Stewart, she feigned to strike him. Alan stepped in and put his hand up to stop. Angie then wiped away a tear. Composing herself, she continued, 'I thought I had perhaps seen you . . . so you were there all the time. And I have had my own kind of hell with you gone. How could you do that to me?' She was asking this again, with her hand resting on her now considerable bump.

Alan then spoke. 'Look, Stewart, what is this all about? This is one hell of a shock.'

Stewart took off his raincoat and reverently placed it on a bar stool. He started to move forward and others moved out of his way as he walked. Stewart then selected an easy chair and leant against it with his arms outstretched. He looked at the assembled mass. Where would he start?

He then spoke. 'I am truly sorry. I am sorry for everything. That life I once led, the deception. But the secret world is over now.' He looked towards Angie. 'I am here for you now, Angie. I know about the baby and the father but I don't care, you see. I want to take responsibility, with you that is.'

Angie reached for a tissue under the sleeve of her cardigan and wiped her eyes before she replied, 'God knows Stewart, it is what I want, but why did we have to go through all of this pain? The funeral and all those mourning. You will tell me next you were there at the church that very day! All this deceit for what?'

'All I can say is that I am deeply sorry. I am here for you if that is what you want.'

Angie paused and sighed. 'Yes, yes, it is what I have wanted, for sure.'

It was at that point that the two armed police officers arrived. Edmund was ready by the door, as he himself had planned, and pointed Stewart out to them. Unlike in the movies, the scene of Stewart's arrest was relatively benign. Edmund had been asked to place his right arm on the target's shoulder to ensure positive identification. He did so silently and calmly, with Stewart staring intently at him. With the betrayal effected, an officer carrying an automatic pistol walked in slowly, with measured steps.

'Blimey!' said Oscar. 'It's like a scene from a TV drama in here now!'

Undaunted by the attempt at humour, the first officer spoke. 'Stewart Lee, you are to now place your hands down and turn to me.' Stewart did so. Then the other officer moved forward and in one swift move clipped Stewart's hands into a plastic tie. One of the team close by Stewart gasped. Stewart was then subjected to a body search, after which the first officer nodded to the other.

Another person then entered but was not in uniform. She spoke in measured tones first to Edmund and then to Stewart about the jurisdiction of the Prevention of Terrorism Act. Stewart was to be detained for a non-designated period of time, and so on, but he seemed not to be paying attention.

Is this how my father felt – was this what he experienced? Stewart now remembered his mother telling him about the letter she had received from the HK Government. It contained an executive order under the Emergency Regulations 1967. It was addressed to B. Lee himself but delivered to their own home: *You are to be detained* was how the order began and further down the word *indefinitely* appeared.

The intelligence officer seemed to be making sense to him again. There was a mention of a right to seek legal advice on the situation he now found himself in. Then she continued and referred Stewart's attention to the car outside. Stewart turned to Edmund as he walked by, flanked by the police officers.

'Edmund, it's fine. I understand. I want you to know that I had decided to give myself up in any event. I knew you had found out.'

Edmund looked at Stewart and briefly nodded. Stewart turned to the gathering: 'To you all, you won't see me for some time but I am back with you.' Stewart was led away. A gust of wind blew the oak tree so that its leaves swayed back and forth over the waiting car. It seemed to approve of the night's events.

At that moment the rain stopped.

When Stewart was led away to the car, his head was held upright, looking almost triumphant. This was not the normal image of an arrested or a condemned man. He walked towards the official vehicle and turned to the pavilion as its door was opened. The team plus all the other guests had now gathered by the steps. Stewart was not concerned if they felt ill of him. He had been true to himself. He now had to submit to the verdict of another type of umpire, this time with a wig and sitting in a courtroom. Out or Not Out, that would be the question.

When that time came, only the judge and lawyers were present. The proceedings were *in camera* and were heard at the Law Courts on the Strand. Stewart had his counsel with him, and Angie, and so felt that he was not entirely alone against the State. Something or someone was with him there, and he felt oddly content. Offered the final chance to make amends and work in the future exclusively for his now adopted country, he agreed to the terms presented by the court. There would be considerable debriefing, further training assessments and the like. But it would be familiar to him. After all he was an old spy, too late to change all his habits. An electronic tag would have to be worn for a period but no other form of punishment handed down to him. Stewart was free to walk outside the courtroom and his handcuffs were removed.

It was, for the moment at least, all about Angie and the child. This was his life now. Although he had lived many times before, he considered that this particular life was the one that he would choose for himself. He walked outside a free man.

Some witnesses said they heard the shot. Others nearer to Stewart only heard the loud thud of his body hitting the floor. Angie's anguished screams resonated around the walls of the judges' car park outside the courts in a small open courtyard. The shooter, gender unknown, fired an automatic pistol from the pavement on Fleet Street. The person was wearing a brown hoodie hiding the face and then calmly stepped on to the back of a motorbike waiting outside St Clement Danes. It raced the wrong way down the street as the bells of St Clement's rang out 12 o'clock.